MW01611047

Copyright: March, 2015

Cover Design: The Killion Group, Inc.
Nancy Brophy
ISBN: 978-0-9862354-3-6

Contact Nancy at: www.NancyBrophy.com
NancyBrophy@gmail.com

The Wrong Series

Each SEAL team member has a core belief that has led him to become the best of the best. No one becomes a SEAL for public adoration. Acknowledgment doesn't happen, at least not on an individual level. Becoming a SEAL team member is almost impossible. Only a very few achieve it.

Once in, the decision to leave is gut wrenching. If one chooses to not make the Navy a lifetime commitment, then who is he? Who will he become? Will he ever achieve the same satisfaction, beyond being an adrenaline junkie, in another career?

This series is about men who are ex-SEALs or in the case Zack Pritchard, on their way out. These are stories of men who struggle to transfer their beliefs, values and training into careers as private civilians while retaining the same sense of dedication and honor.

Book 2, The Wrong Hero, is the story of Travis Stevens a man who transitioned easily from SEAL team leader to co-owner of a private corporate security firm. But while Travis may know everything about directing his men and later his employees, he knows nothing about making a relationship work.

Book 1 –
The Wrong Brother
Zack and Chloe

This is what lying got you – the wrong brother.

Book 2 –
The Wrong Hero
Travis and Abby

"If this is a chess game, the one thing you should have been able to predict is that the queen always protects the king.

Book 3 –
The Wrong Cop
Grant and Dori

"It pisses me off I'm attracted to you." His erection betrayed his words.

He was lying, but so was she. "You're like the wad of gum on the sole of my shoe. Only worth as much consideration as it takes to get rid of you."

Book 3.5 - Bonus book –
The Wrong Lover
Marshall and Lily

Her brown eyes and raspy voice stayed with him. Her taste lingered on his lips. After this fiasco was over, he'd find her. All he knew was that her name was Lily, but it wasn't her name he was after.

Book 4 –
THE WRONG HUSBAND
Austin and Nicole

"It's a vacation and we are going to have a fabulous time."

Book 5 –
THE WRONG SEAL
Sam and Imogene

She had no idea how lucky she'd been to be raised in a place where crazy people weren't running the circus.

Chapter One

Tuesday
Portland, Oregon

"Charrrrleee."

The high-pitched, alcohol-induced giggle pulled Pierce Johnson's attention from his computer monitor. The only 'Charlie' on this end of the floor was Charles Weatherby Stewart, III; the Harvard-educated lawyer and senior partner in Staunton, Lambo, and Stewart.

The past nine months of Pierce's life had been spent in drudgery, working eighty to a hundred hours a week as an intern directly under the senior partner's supervision. And while the partners made hundreds of thousands of dollars, first year interns waiting on the bar exam could barely pay the rent.

"Charrrrleee," the sing-song chant came again, "where are you?"

Pierce checked the time. Nine P.M. At this hour only a handful of employees remained—more interns than lawyers. And not a single individual who wished to see sunshine the next day called Charles Weatherby Stewart, III, 'Charlie.'

Pierce clicked an obscure icon on his crowded computer screen and the pictures from the hidden webcam in Stewart's office came into view. Bugging his boss's office had been a stroke of genius, but he'd never expected to see something like this.

Staunton, Lambo, and Stewart was widely considered the top corporate firm in the entire Pacific Northwest. According to conventional wisdom if you made it here, your career was set for life. After nine months, Pierce believed if you made it with SLS, you were too demoralized to go anywhere else.

"Here you are!" The brunette's delighted squeal bounced off the walls as she flounced into Mr. Stewart's office. Her short sequined dress sparkled in the dim light, and her sugar tits threatened to spill out of the low-cut bodice.

"How much did you cost, baby?" Pierce asked the monitor. "Charlie, you have been very naughty. To think I've taken every ounce of shit you've dished out. Finally, it's payback time."

The brunette sidled between the desk and Stewart's chair, hoisted herself onto his desk and spread her legs. "Happy birthday."

Stewart's manicured fingers curled around her fleshy open inner thighs.

The muscles in Pierce's throat worked overtime to keep from drooling. "Oh, yeah. That's a money shot."

He'd give anything to see his boss's expression, but the camera's angle was directed toward Charles's computer rather than his face. Pierce snickered. This view was too good to give up.

"Are you sure you're in the right place? Not my birthday…." Stewart's deep voice sounded distracted.

Pierce snickered. He doubted words were necessary as he leaned closer to the scene. A small crow of laughter escaped as he whispered, "C'mon, boss. Let's see some technique."

"It's not your birthday?" She tilted her head. Long, curly brunette tresses tumbled in front of the monitor and obscured the light. Pierce squinted, trying to see her face, but the darkness hid her features.

"Jonas sent a gift."

Pierce's screen went black. "What—"

He jiggled the monitor. Instead of images, occasional flashes light were accompanied by a scuffling noise.

A moment of silence followed, broken by the woman's words, "Jesus, you got blood all over me. I thought you were going to snap his neck, not slit his throat." A stronger no-nonsense voice replaced the baby-doll tones.

Pierce leaped out of his seat and jumped backward, gasping, as he tried to suck oxygen into his lungs without success. Blood? Slit his throat?

A gruff, masculine voice Pierce didn't recognize, asked. "Did you see anyone?"

As quickly as he'd backed away, Pierce leaned forward over the desk to peer at the screen mere inches from his nose. Too many pixels — not enough pixels. He couldn't determine anything.

"I'll look around and get cleaned up." Her casual tone alarmed him.

They'd killed once. Another murder wouldn't be out of the realm of possibilities. He was the only other person at this end of the hall.

Pierce rushed to the door and flipped the deadbolt while Miss Candypants rattled off instructions. "Grab his computer and search his pockets."

Was she in charge or the man? And what did it mean that she was going to look around? Where? Small hairs on the back of his neck stood on end. He squirmed to relieve the sensation of spiders crawling up his back.

His door was dead-bolted. Little good that would do.

The firm's security maintained that the entire end of the hall be secured behind doors required key cards and passcodes, then the lawyers and staff left the doors open for convenience.

The individual door locks were more ornamental than substantial, particularly on those door belonging to interns.

His former military uncles were all capable of kicking a door off the hinges. and he bet the people across the hall were, too. Even the woman.

He wiped the sweat from his forehead, knowing his death was imminent. His throat clenched while his stomach threatened to erupt.

He'd selected corporate law in order to be above the fray of common everyday criminals. Instead, he was immersed in blood and gore. Never had he dreamed he'd see his boss, or anybody for that matter, murdered.

Snatching his laptop and cell phone from the desk, he extinguished the dim desk light. Where to go? He searched the small office, looking for a place to hide. With no other alternatives, he crawled under his desk.

Who was in the building? Who could help?

He should dial 9-1-1. Sam, his uncle in-name-only, had lived with them as a kid and was now a detective with the Portland Police. How long would it take him to get here?

Pierce gnawed his lower lip. What if he got arrested for bugging Stewart's office? Of all his relatives, Sam towed a strict line. His intolerance for scofflaws had been the source of many family dinner arguments.

His mother would disown him if he were arrested. He'd lose his job.

Sam's partner, Grant was a good guy, but he was a single dad with a sick baby. Sam would have his hide if he got Grant to come rescue Pierce on his off-hours. Calling the police was a bad idea. He needed another plan

Travis and Austin, his step-uncles were in private security only a few blocks away. One of them was always working late. They'd help him, but either or both would rat him out to Sam. It'd be three against one, except they'd talk Sam out of an arrest. But it would come at a price – like giving them a license to constantly meddle in his life.

Why hadn't Pierce thought about this when he installed the webcam? At the time, it seemed like such a good idea. The last thing he expected was for the police to get involved. And he sure as hell had never expected murder.

He hung his head as he tried to get a handle on what to do.

Then it came to him. He could call Trey. She always had great ideas. She'd figure a way out of this.

Chapter Two

Travis Stevens pushed end call on his cell phone and turned to his dinner date. Unable to remember her name, he leaned across the narrow table and patted the busty blonde's hand. He guessed her to be about his age – thirty-four – but a million years of life lay between them.

"I'm sorry. An emergency—" He stopped. Giving an explanation wasted time. "Gotta go."

The woman blinked. Her mascara-laden eyelashes batted her cheeks. Travis kept his expression level as he had for the past hour and forty minutes. Make that forty-two minutes. God save him from well-meaning friends who were convinced he needed to "get back on the horse again" and start dating.

Dating had never been his thing. But he'd agreed to go. And had listened as she emptied her heart about her emotionally clingy mother, her psycho ex, and her dog's surgery.

Her only redeeming trait was a great rack. She'd paid for a nice set of tits, and showcased them in a sexy halter dress for his benefit. In return, he silently praised her plastic surgeon.

He rose without waiting for her response and tossed three twenties onto the table to cover their wine and a decent tip.

She drained her glass and glanced at her watch before standing. "You have my phone number." Annoyance tinged her tone.

He shook his head. "I'm not ready to date yet. You're parked near here?"

A well-practiced pout crossed her face, but Travis didn't have time to smooth hurt feelings. He'd lost enough time. Pierce was in trouble.

Due to the trendy neighborhood, his Escalade was several blocks away in the wrong direction. The US Bank Tower was nearby. He estimated his run time at about twelve minutes, but first he had to get his date at least to the door. She handed him her coat. and he resisted the urge to shove her arms inside.

Instead of walking with purpose, she ambled, forcing him to put a firm hand to the small of her back to hurry her along. Outside, she lingered, clinging to his arm.

He gently disengaged her hand, refusing to acknowledge her disappointed expression. "Gotta go." Without waiting for a reply, he darted across the street, weaving through heavy traffic and set off at a run.

Not even out of breath, he entered the almost empty lobby eleven minutes later, skirted the vacant night-security desk and headed for the banks of elevators. Only one at the far end stood open.

A rhythmic tapping slowed his pace as a young blind woman rounded the corner. Her white cane marked her steady progress on the marble floor. A profusion of blonde ringlets topped her head and dark, wrap-around sunglasses covered her eyes. An outstretched hand found the call button. After a moment of fumbling she pressed the top one. The open elevator dinged.

Despite his hurry, he couldn't resist offering help. "This one's open." He extended his hand only to realize she couldn't see it. While he would have preferred to go it alone, he refused to take the only elevator and leave her stranded.

When she reached the door, he clasped her upper arm to steer her inside and hurry along her progress.

She stopped and whirled toward him, speaking to his chest. "Did I ask for your help?"

The frosty tones conveyed her annoyance. He should have known better. He'd spent too many years in the military not to understand an injury would not make a proud person dependent.

"Sorry."

He steeled his patience and waited for her to enter. She stationed herself in front of the key panel, fingering the Braille markings designating each floor. Independence and pride were important, but so was time.

He reached above her outstretched arm and pushed the number nineteen, then asked, "Floor?"

"Twenty."

Her tone had eased. Apparently his apology worked. Now a sexy, honey-laced voice clenched his spine and sent spikes of heat shooting through his body. He took another look at the woman whose spirit he admired.

Mid-thirties, but she appeared younger with all that blonde, curly hair. Her perfume smelled sultry, probably one he'd seen advertised with a come-on name, like Hot Desire or Do Me, Daddy.

"Thank you."

There it was again. Her voice made his body ache. Since his divorce, his interest in the opposite sex had all but disappeared, but now, it roared back to life. And his interest wasn't the only thing rearing its head. Automatically he buttoned his jacket before it occurred to him a blind woman wouldn't be able to detect the bulge in his slacks.

Instead he stepped to the opposite front corner but angled his body to monitor her movements. With ramrod straight posture, she faced the keypad. When he tapped his foot in impatience, she looked at the floor in the direction of his shoes.

"Sorry." He'd apologized more to her in the past two minutes, than to anyone in the past year. Perfect. He forced himself to stop fidgeting.

His years as a SEAL had taught him patience and had anyone, but his nephew been in trouble, he would have been calmer. His friends and co-workers were men like himself – competent, intense warriors who protected the weak and disenfranchised, armed with an inherent hatred of those who picked on women and children. He had grown up in a household that had given him firsthand experience with abuse and terror. His number one goal was to spare others from the nightmare he'd experienced.

And while Pierce was no longer a child, he'd been a small, nerdy kid who was bullied and tormented throughout school. His mother – Travis' stepsister – was an egghead full of arcane facts. Her son was smart but veered toward incompetence. Opening a childproof medicine bottle required safety cones. The fact he'd chosen to huddle under his desk during a crisis spoke of a man mollycoddled. The finger of blame rested firmly at Travis' overprotective door.

The bell dinged for his floor. The woman pivoted her head as though she could see into the corridor. He restrained himself from lurching out the door, not wanting to alert her to a problem. But before the door was completely open, she raised her palm in the universal symbol for stop.

"Can I help you, ma'am?" an official-sounding male voice asked. Crisp. Authoritative. Military background.

Travis's senses tingled, jolting him into a battle readiness while his brain worked to put pieces into place. Had she warned him because she heard people in the hall? His hearing was excellent, but maybe hers was better. He sensed danger – did she as well?

The woman had something. Clever women worried him because their agenda wasn't readily apparent.

He faded into the front corner of the elevator while the blind woman straddled the threshold and reached high on the wall to feel the number nineteen posted on the outside door frame. Her skirt rose with her hand. Under normal circumstances, he would have admired the view, but enough exposed thigh might encourage the other man closer. He pressed further into the wall.

"Dammit, wrong floor. I hate it when I do that."

"Do you want help?" The voice had neared.

Travis slipped his hand inside his jacket and wrapped his fingers around his HK.

"I can get it." Those icy tones she'd perfected snapped with annoyance. "It's hard enough to be blind without feeling like a cripple, too."

Her words put the other man in his place and

hopefully stopped him from approaching.

"You should get a dog."

Travis suppressed a disbelieving chuckle. Not a woman he would have offered that advice.

Her blonde curls bounced as she hopped impatiently on her heel.

He crowded the front corner, gun drawn. Glad she was blind and he wouldn't have to worry that she'd panic at the sight of a weapon.

She punched the twentieth-floor button, then discreetly dropped her hand to push the close door button. "Really? Do you think a dog could read the numbers better than I can?"

The door closed on a startled guffaw from the hall.

As the elevator rose, the tension in Travis' neck and shoulders eased. "Thanks."

She held up her hand to stop him a second time. On the next floor, they stepped out. "Elevator shaft sound carries," she said in an almost whisper. "If those yo-yos heard a masculine voice, they would have come to investigate."

"How many were there?" Why the hell was he asking a blind woman a visual question?

"Two," she answered without pausing, tossing her dark glasses into her bag. "The second man kept turning to check what was going on further down the hall."

Okay, not so blind. The white cane snapped into pieces like a carpenter's ruler. Her blonde curls turned out to be a wig, which disappeared along with the cane into her oversized purse.

His need to get to his nephew waned as the

blonde, now brunette, transformed. She tugged on black pants, unhooked her skirt, then stepped out of the circle of fabric that floated to the floor. She stashed it in her bag, before exchanging the four-inch heels for rubber-soled flats. Her movements were swift and efficient.

She finger-combed her dark locks into some kind of order. Never once had he used the word 'tousled' and yet that was the perfect word to describe her hair. With her generously lashed chocolate eyes and soft, pale lips, she was by far the sexiest woman he'd ever seen. Had the transformation not happened in front of him, he would never have guessed the women were one and the same.

Her pants and shirt fit snug. He admired the view while searching for weapons.

"Are you staring at my ass?"

His gaze met hers, and he grinned, then ventured a guess. "You're here for Pierce?"

"Of course."

Had Pierce called in a team? There was no 'of course' here, but before he could mention that fact, she focused on him, and he fumbled his next question.

She chatted casually like time wasn't of the essence. "You're one of his relatives, aren't you? I told him to call you. Are you Travis or Austin? I know you're not Sam."

A cold hand of warning closed around his throat. How did this woman know so much about his family? "Travis."

"I thought so. I understand Austin looks quite young. Pierce talks about you all the time." She rummaged through her purse as she spoke. "I've got lipstick in here somewhere."

A flush of shame darkened his heart. He'd never noticed Pierce was interested in women. Well, to be fair, he wasn't interested in men, either. At least not that Travis had seen. He'd pegged the kid as a loner, certainly not a man dating a woman who had to be at least nine or ten years older. Pierce, the egghead, had a girlfriend. And she was a cougar who came prepared with a costume change. How unusual was that?

"You had all this stuff with you?" he asked, trying not to gape.

"Long story." She pulled out her phone and texted briefly. "I'm telling him we are here, but there are people all over the floor and to stay hidden."

"Don't send it. His phone will ding."

"Not if he turned his volume off like I told him."

Her phone dinged a second later. After she had read the message, she said. "He's safe. No one had tried to enter his office. He heard voices in the hallway a few minutes ago, but they've faded."

She opened the door to the stairwell. "As soon as the door latches, try to come back in."

Travis hesitated. She thought she was in charge? When had he stepped into this world of insanity? He'd been in command so long he couldn't imagine anyone usurping his authority much less a younger woman he outweighed by eighty pounds.

"Why?" He treaded cautiously, wanting to know more about her before he revealed his skills.

"So we don't get locked in the stairway."

Travis stepped past her into the stairwell, reached around the door, and flicked the handle a couple of times. The bolt retracted each time.

"See?" he said. "No problem." He didn't tell her a locked door wouldn't have slowed him down. Where had she gotten her training? When had she met his nephew? Now he had to keep this woman safe while he rescued both. What in the world had Pierce been thinking? Travis needed to reemphasize that men did not invite their girlfriends to potentially dangerous situations.

When the door didn't lock, she entered the stairwell and actually allowed him to go first. He was pleased to note she maneuvered the concrete stairs as quietly as he did. At the nineteenth-floor door, she thrust a small curved mirror in his direction.

Really? Had Pierce portrayed him as incompetent? Certainly he'd called for backup. A mirror? What kind of covert op did she think this was? Knowing Pierce was currently safe, allowed him to revamp his plan.

He bit back his laughter. She'd had some fun at his expense with the fake blind girl thing. It was time for a turnaround. He held the mirror eye-level and nodded. "I look good."

The outrage on her face was priceless, but before she could tell him what she thought of his humor, he grabbed her arms and whipped her body against the wall. His pride was assuaged when she trembled.

"Who trained you?"

Perspiration beaded above her upper lip. Faint freckles skied across her nose while the combination of heat, soft woman and witchy scent wrapped around his spine and pressed him closer.

"Trained me?" Her blank expression lasted only a couple of seconds. "No one. I'm a mystery writer. We think about these things."

Was she kidding? A mystery writer? No way.

"Why did you have a disguise at your fingertips?"

She pursed her lips. His instinct was to kiss them, but he held himself back, knowing that would just be the beginning. He longed to taste her, explore her body, discover her mysteries, writer or not.

"My current WIP features a heroine who's a cat burglar. I practice to get the details right."

She pushed off from the wall, but he refused to budge. Not until he got answers. But in her struggle, her body bumped into his – nice and hard.

Oh, yeah, honey. Let's do that again.

He forced his focus to her answer. "WIP?"

"Work in progress."

Her voice betrayed exasperation as though he should have known what she meant. He'd spent his life around dangerous men, but this woman scared him. She played games with other people's lives. Writing wasn't real, and this was a job where a pen was no match for a gun. No way could he let her enter the corridor.

He paused, wanting to gain a clear perspective. She was clever. He had truly believed she was blind, and she had protected him in the elevator. What other tricks did she have in mind?

"Do you have a plan?"

Her perfume teased his nostrils and wove a lasso through the portion of his brain she hadn't yet stolen. She was like a juicy peach he longed to bite. Her breath came in short spurts, and her cheeks flushed a pretty shade of pink. The pulse in her neck jumped.

She shook her head. "Pierce is nervous under normal situations. After this, he'll be a basket case. Once everyone's left, I figured I'd be the one to make sure he got safely home."

Well, that was true enough. Travis was tempted to soften his opinion of her, but he needed more information.

"Good idea." His response was curt. It made sense to drop it there, but he couldn't let one nagging thought go. "You know Pierce how?"

"Landlady. Pierce rents half a duplex from me."

His landlady? Could this situation get any more bizarre? Travis feared saying the words aloud because the answer might be yes.

"What's your name?

"My friends call me Trey."

"Real name?"

"Abigail Brooks."

"You're not his girlfriend?" He had to know. He could not imagine being attracted to a woman dating Pierce. And he was definitely interested. His entire body was a blaze of need. How long had it been since a woman affected him like this?

"Date Pierce?" She scowled. Those sultry brown eyes squinted as she tried to read his face. "What's wrong with you? When I decide to take off my clothes and get naked with a man, it's at least going to be someone who's been around the park bench more than once — and on a side note — weighs more than I do."

He pushed away from her and looked down. It was strictly for effect. He'd already admired the shape of her ass and her long legs in the dress and heels. Now he took a leisurely perusal to let her feel his heat.

"There's nothing wrong with your body." His voice was gruffer than he intended. His plan had been to make her uncomfortable, not betray how interested he was.

She rolled her eyes in mock annoyance. "You're not my type either."

He masked his response at the woman's audacity with a disbelieving cough. "Liar. You may not want to like me, but your scent tells me your body's already thinking about getting naked."

Her face flushed crimson.

He wanted to kiss her but didn't have time. Kissing her would not be quick, and she was a woman who needed proper kissing. Instead he wedged his leg between hers, pressing as high as her clenched thighs would allow. "What weapons are you carrying?"

Chapter Three

"Weapons? I'm a writer. I've got a ballpoint pen and a highlighter." Abby wanted to sound indignant, but at the same time she considered his words. A weapon would be a good idea. Her heroines were always armed.

Jeez, if he'd back up and give her a little breathing room she could think better. His car was on the starting line, gunning the motor, and her engine was revving right along with his. When Pierce talked about his uncle he'd never mentioned, the man was take-your-breathe-away hot.

Her comment about getting naked had been a mistake. Now all she could think about was sliding between the sheets with him. She bet when he took off his clothes females everywhere, even blind ones, would applaud.

She'd never written a hero as hunky as Travis. Her hands clung to his steely upper arms. She should take photos so she'd remember how to describe his body. And that leg that pushed between hers.... The upward crook of his mouth assured her that any surreptitious desires she harbored were not that secret.

She wriggled to get out of his grip, but all she succeeded into doing was to press her inseam against his thigh.

Oooh... Don't do that again. At least now right now...

She couldn't do this. She couldn't agree to an affair. A sigh escaped her lips.

"Here's the plan." His deep voice, even softly spoken, brought her back to reality.

Rescue Pierce. But she was the one in need of a life preserver.

Focus — on the nephew — not the uncle.

Pierce claimed his Uncle Travis was the man in charge. That was as understated as calling an iceberg a small peak in the water.

"I'm going to make sure our boy's safe while you call the police." His gaze studied her face while he outlined his ideas. "Ask for Detective Sam Sampson, or if he's tied up, his partner, Grant Matthews. Pierce said he bugged his boss' office or something hair-brained like that, so I'll have to look for the tape. The kid's lost his mind with this little trick."

Oh, shit. Pierce had taken her seriously?

Travis's arm tightened around her waist. "What?"

This was not going to be good. Well, she needed to get rid of him anyway. The truth, which had never worked for her in the past, was suddenly a beacon of light.

"I might have mentioned to Pierce that in my book, *Stolen Money, Stolen Lives*, my heroine used a webcam to discover her boss was embezzling."

He eased his upper body back, but his leg remained firmly lodged between hers. Even worse, his movement shifted his thigh higher.

She squeezed her eyes closed. *His naked shoulder and neck were poised above her in bed as he slowly drove himself forward---*

"Stewart was embezzling?"

She shook her head, inching further against the wall and reluctantly opened her eyes. "No. Pierce was concerned about his status."

Her breasts ached. She didn't dare look down for

fear of drawing his gaze. She needed to calm down, but that would be impossible with his thigh stroking hers.

Travis frowned. Pewter eyes turned to cold steel. The chiseled lines in his face hardened.

Not a man she'd have chosen to piss off. "He bugged his boss's office to find out if he was getting a promotion?" His words were harsh with judgment.

She shrugged. Personally she was surprised Pierce had shown the balls to do anything besides fret, but saying that to the guy's uncle would be another mistake, and she'd already made too many this evening.

He stepped back taking his heat with him. Bereft, her body yearned. She fisted her fingers to keep from pulling him back into her arms.

But she read the distance in his eyes. He was already on step three of his plan. "You stay here. I'm going to find Pierce."

Alone? Panic rose in her throat as the reality of his words slammed home. "Aren't we a team?"

He grinned, warming his eyes and easing the sharpness of his face. She'd considered him ruggedly handsome, but now he was an approachable semi-gorgeous hunk. Every cell in her body stood up and took notice, which she wouldn't have thought was possible.

"Oh, yeah, we're a team, baby. I'm executing the rescue. Your job is to provide a distraction, which you did."

"What if they come this way?"

"Try the blind woman falling down the stairs. I think they'll buy that. I did."

The door closed. She was alone. Like always. She clutched her waist. What would a kick-ass heroine do?

Well, a heroine wouldn't waste time longing for a man who'd left her to fend for herself, that's for sure. Neither would Abby. And since she never had before, why start now?

She paused and took a deep breath. If this was one of her stories, what would the heroine do? How would she get the villains out of the action?'

They weren't worried about being seen which meant they'd probably hacked into the security system and disabled the cameras.

What did every crime need? A get-away vehicle, of course.

Would they use underground parking at this time of night? Only one way to find out.

She hoofed her way to the eighteenth floor and stuck her head into the corridor. No one was around. After dashing out the door and around the corner, she punched the button for the elevator. So much faster when one wasn't blind.

P1 and P2 were the parking levels. A get-away car would be as close to the exit as possible. But what would they drive? Not a sedan. Something big. After all, there were at least four, maybe five of them. Six, if they had a driver.

Parking level one was almost empty. On parking level two she found a large suburban and a paneled van. Not very original. She scoffed. If she turned in something so clichéd, her editor would have kicked it back.

She held her head high, and with a purposeful stride, crossed behind the two vehicles. Her pulse pounded in her ears, but her neck was stiff, making her surveillance attempt awkward. She wished she carried a briefcase rather than an oversized purse. Was she being watched? Did she look as if she belonged in the building?

What would she do if someone leaped out? Run like hell, screaming all the way. Surprisingly, even that simple plan was enough to slow her racing heart

The license plates were mud-covered, but the word Idaho was clearly visible. The vehicles were empty, but the men from the nineteenth floor could appear at any minute, making her afraid to get close enough to scrape the mud. Instead, she ducked behind a concrete pillar. The elevator dinged, echoing in the concrete garage.

Whipping out her cell phone she took photos of both vehicles and license plates. In her stories, her heroes always had cool tracking devices. Wouldn't it be handy to hide one on each vehicle now?

She placed her camera on video and focused it in the direction of the elevator. The very least she could do was get a shot of them leaving. The men in the hallway had been wearing all black with tightly wrapped Kevlar vests, combat boots, and heavy utility belts.

What had a top-flight attorney done to merit being killed? Between sobs, Pierce had mumbled that they were hunting for something. What would corporate lawyers know that would put someone in danger?

Information. Duh.

Stewart had known something he shouldn't.

The elevator opened. She stilled her instinct to jump back. Three men exited accompanied by a woman dressed as a party girl. From behind the post, Abby studied the female, confident all that hair was a wig, and her toned body wasn't achieved through pole dancing.

The three men marched in perfect step as if on military parade. The woman double stepped to keep up. No one spoke. Something about the woman caught Abby's eye, and it wasn't her impossibly high heels. She favored her right leg ever so slightly. The man on her right offered an arm, but the woman brushed it off. The men headed for the SUV while the woman opened the van's side door. Why two vehicles?

Shit. Abby had forgotten to call the police. She dialed 9-1-1 as the taillights disappeared at the far end of the garage.

"9-1-1. What is your emergency?"

"Please put me through to the police."

"I'm sorry ma'am. This is 9-1-1, not the police switchboard. Is this an emergency?"

"Well, not anymore since they just got away. Never mind." She punched end call with her thumb.

She gritted her teeth, pacing the garage not wanting to confess she'd botched her one assignment. So much for her participation as a team member.

She'd stalled enough and reluctantly turned toward the elevator. Even while her mind urged her body to hurry, each step of the twenty feet was sluggishly slow. The elevator, however, zipped to the nineteenth floor. Naturally at this time of night there would be nothing to slow it down. She took one final deep breath to prepare herself to face an angry Travis Stevens.

The door opened to reveal an empty corridor, except for the uniformed officer standing at the far end. His attention was focused on the open door of another office. So the police had arrived even without her call. They must have missed the killers by seconds. Travis was nowhere to be seen. She followed the directions Pierce had given her to his office.

The handle gave easily, but his workstation was mostly dark, lit by the night sky from windows and the artificial light from the hall fixture behind her.

"Pierce?" she whispered into the room.

"Trey?" an equally soft voice responded. His voice was young and tentative, breaking her heart. He had been panicked while she'd devoted all her energies to playing footsie with his uncle.

Abby moved inside, closing the door firmly behind her. "It's me. Where are you?" A chair bumped the wall. A shadow emerged. "Where's the light?"

A dim desk lamp clicked on, allowing her to see his frightened face, devoid of color. "I unlocked the door once I knew you were here."

She glanced at the office scarcely larger than a cubicle. An expensive camel-haired coat hung on the rack next to the door. "Let's go home."

Pierce managed a terse nod, reached across the desk and plunged the room into darkness. Abby opened the door, so light from the hall provided a path. She grabbed the coat and thrust it toward him. "Put this on."

He shook his head. Abby bit her lips. He would want his coat in the morning. She tossed it over her arm. The hall previously littered with police was now empty. She held his arm for support as they entered the elevator. "You'll feel better after a hot bath."

Chapter Four

Wednesday Morning

The pounding on Abby's door woke her from a sound sleep. She stubbed her toe on the nightstand, groping for the light switch. The shift from dark to light temporarily blinded her. Closing her eyes, she hoped it wasn't morning because her body wasn't ready to get up.

With that thought in mind, she snatched her cell phone from the charging cradle and stomped down the stairs to the front door.

12:26 AM. This had better be a dire emergency.

Before she flung open the door, she stopped. What if this was Agent Stern? How could he know what happened? But he always knew. And he appeared when she least expected it.

Inhaling sharply, she leaned against the doorframe. "Who is it?"

"Pierce."

The breath she'd been holding billowed out. Her renter merely looked sleepy, but he was flanked by his snarling uncle.

Good to see you, too.

Another man stood at the rear. Despite the jacket and tie, he had the bearing of a cop. No doubt the Detective "Sam" Sampson, or perhaps this was the partner, Grant something.

"Do come in." She hoped her sarcasm wouldn't be lost on the men. "Can I get you coffee?"

"Trey makes the world's best coffee," Pierce spoke as though this was a social call. "She has this neat trick where she puts just a touch of cinnamon in the pot."

Abby clamped her mouth closed. Pierce's rent was due for an increase next month. Let's see how he felt about her coffee when she gave him that bill.

Detective Sampson must have read her face correctly because he shook her hand and mumbled his name. "It's late."

"You're here. I'm going back to bed." Pierce turned to leave, but Sam clasped his hand around his neck.

"You in enough trouble as it is. If I have questions, I don't want to go hunting for you. Sit down and don't talk unless I ask you a question."

Whether it was the tone of his voice or the familiar way he handled Pierce, Abigail realized Sam was no stranger. He was the man, Pierce referred to as 'my uncle in-name-only.'

Travis didn't interfere, choosing instead to lean against the door jamb with his arms folded and silently watch the interaction between the other two.

Sam half-shoved Pierce through the door. "Can we sit at your table?"

"Sure." Abby's drowsiness had left. She was wide awake. Coffee sounded better than it had a minute ago.

Travis sauntered in last, eyeing her sleepwear as he crossed the threshold. "Hockey fan?"

The Blackhawk's jersey covered her body to about mid-thigh. "Used to be."

He raised an eyebrow. "What happened?"

"I got a life."

She dead-bolted the door and turned to catch Travis's lips twitch as he hid his grin.

She couldn't afford to like him.

If Agent Stern found out she'd let a man into her life, everyone here could be in danger.

Gritting her teeth, she gestured the way to the dining room table where Sam and Pierce had already settled.

Travis clutched her upper arm as though she planned to make a run for safety, and he didn't dare let her out of his sight.

"You and Pierce left the scene before we were finished." His tone was accusatory, veering toward anger.

Anger she could handle. It created a much-needed barrier between them.

She was tired, cranky and sorry she'd agreed to help. Pierce and his overbearing uncle hadn't needed or appreciated what she'd done.

She glared. If he thought his job was to boss her around, he'd find out just how mistaken he was.

"My team duties, as you pointed out, were to be a distraction and get Pierce home safely. I did my job. As. Assigned. By. You." She jerked her arm away and dropped onto a chair with considerably less grace than she would have preferred. Well, two men and a boy. "No one told us not to go. You knew Pierce's address."

Detective Sampson held up his hand to stop the retort that was sure to come. Growling, Travis occupied the only empty chair across from hers and folded his arms over his massive chest.

Sampson leveled a withering glance in his direction, which had some effect. At least Travis quit glaring and had the grace to look slightly ashamed.

"I need to ask a few questions," Sam said,

switching to a calm voice designed to defuse the tension.

Abby nodded, feeling more than a little chagrined.

"Your name."

"Abigail Lorraine Brooks."

"The third?"

"No." She frowned before it occurred to her what he asked. "My non-de-plume is Miss Trey Sleuth. Most of my friends call me Trey."

"You're Miss Trey Sleuth?" The detective's interest picked up. His face morphed into the first genuine smile she'd seen since the men arrived. "I've read all your books. My favorite was…" He snapped his fingers several times in rapid succession. "*Murder Under the Bleachers*."

She couldn't help herself, she grinned. "Thanks."

It was nice to receive praise for one's work even in the middle of the night. Not to mention, he had good taste. *Murder Under the Bleachers* was one of her best sellers.

"Miss Trey Sleuth? Mystery Sleuth?" Travis's jaw dropped as he gawked in disbelief. "That's the name you write under?"

Not all of them were on the same page.

Abby raised an eyebrow, ignored Travis's posturing and turned a polite face toward Sam. "Questions?"

He nodded obviously as eager as she to stay on topic. "How long have you known Pierce?"

"He's rented the other half of the duplex for two years."

"So, you're his landlady?"

Pierce, whose head had been resting on the table as though asleep, suddenly came to life. "And my friend."

She favored him with a warm smile.

Sam brushed over the exchange and continued. "Does anyone else live here?"

"Not currently."

He sat with a silence that some men acquire, designed to make one squirm or confess. After all, he was a detective. When she refused to be intimated, he thinned his lips, "Clarify."

Abby gestured casually with her right hand. "I've owned this place for about seven years. I've had other renters, but no one else has lived on my side."

One corner of Travis's lips quirked upward.

She didn't like the way he looked at her. "No," she wanted to tell him. "I'm not wearing a bra! I was asleep in bed. Stop staring."

She turned her head and shifted in her chair, determined to ignore him, shifting her focus to the detective.

As she restrained her words, she also stilled her fingers that itched to sooth her forehead and stave off her headache.

"So, you're single? Divorced?" The detective glanced at Travis before returning his attention to her.

What could she say? She wasn't even sure she knew the truth anymore. And her latest agreement with the government meant she was forced to give her stock answer, but lying to the police was always a mistake.

"Neither." She clutched the hem of her nightshirt under the table to keep from leaping up and running out of the room.

The detective studied her face for a moment,

before pointing out, "That only leaves married."

She nodded. Every muscle in her body tensed. She must have looked like a poorly wired puppet with her head bobbing in such a wooden fashion. "Yes."

Pierce's head jerked up. He and Travis both wore identical looks of shock on their faces.

"You're married?" Pierce asked his voice a high squeak. Travis said nothing, preferring to glower.

"Yes."

Sam must have realized he was losing control because he spoke again before anyone else could comment. "To whom?"

"Captain James Brooks. US Army." Abby's voice sounded calm and in control which pleased her.

Fortunately, no one could hear her blood pounding through her veins or see her frantic fingers twisting the hem of her nightshirt under the table.

The detective probed. "Active duty?"

"Not anymore." She wasn't giving away one thing more than she had to. Still, she bet Agent Stern would be displeased.

Detective Sampson tapped his pen on the table. "Where does he currently reside?"

"VA Hospital."

The room was silent for a full moment while she studied the wood-grain pattern of her table.

"What time did Pierce call you last night?"

Had Sam given up? The stone of dread in her stomach lifted. As long as the questions didn't pertain to her personally, she'd be okay.

Ten-to-one, Stern already knew what was happening. He'd show up in the morning, unannounced, demanding an explanation as to why there were men in her home. Who were they? Why were they there?

She glanced at her cell. Technically it was morning. When and where would he appear? Her house or the VA bedside, wearing that grim look of disapproval that made her knees quake.

She thought for a moment. Since Stern's appearance was inevitable, the real question remained what had the government done with her husband and who was the man in the hospital bed? Could these men actually help her? Or if she confided in them, would they turn out to be another part of the problem? After all, the police had laughed when she'd gone to them before.

Her gaze shifted to the ceiling and scanned the four corners of the room. The government always knew what she did. Somewhere in this room there were cameras and probably microphones as well. Better to stick to the script.

Travis scooted his chair across her hardwood floor. His patience was on a short fuse and apparently had eroded entirely. He rose and marched around the room, staring at her artwork and handling her possessions. At the far end of the table, Detective Sampson rolled his eyes and returned to his notes.

Since her marriage, men had fallen off her radar. Travis was the first man who managed a blip. And his blip was a bright one. He wore integrity like a suit of armor. How different would her life have turned out if she had met him before James?

Despite her momentary weakness last night, she wasn't available. The government had drummed that into her. The longer these men lingered, the more trouble it would create.

Her attention switched to the detective who now

wore an expectant look. Apparently he'd asked a question, which she missed. "I'm sorry?"

"Travis told you to call me when he left you on the stairs, but you didn't call."

"I got sidetracked." Finally, she could offer something of value to get them out of here. She grabbed her cell and pressed buttons. "In the parking garage."

As soon as the video appeared she pushed her phone toward him. "I can email this to you."

The detective's eyes widened, and a huge grin crossed his face. "These are the guys you saw in the hall?"

She nodded. Travis moved soundlessly from the far side of the room and leaned over the table to view the recording. "Good. A facial shot of the woman. Austin will be pleased."

Goosebumps rose on her skin as Travis's gaze evaluated her.

Sam opened his wallet and pushed his card toward her. "This is great. Here's my email."

Another card landed on top of the first. "And mine." Travis's hand squeezed her shoulder. "Good teamwork, Miss Sleuth."

His words stunned her. How long had it been since a man offered her praise for something other than her stories?

A smile curved her lips, but her eyes stung. This hurt much worse than she'd imagined. She'd sold her soul, and it had never bothered her until this very moment.

Chapter Five

Wednesday Morning

Travis spewed fire. His grip on the steering wheel was so firm the hard plastic under the leather remolded to fit his fingers. He'd been angry last night when Abby and his nephew left the bank tower, leaving Sam no alternative but to follow them home.

His fury had erupted when he realized she'd put herself in danger to get the video, but he'd also been insanely pleased she was so bright and quick-witted. That video was pure gold. It would protect Pierce and help identify the murderers.

But his temper, like Elvis, had left the building when she announced her status − M.A.R.R.I.E.D. to a permanently hospitalized veteran. Travis's life sucked, but it was possible hers was worse.

Austin, his brother and partner in Stevens Securities, remained at the office searching the Internet for clues about Abby and the murderers. While the names Abigail and James Brooks were scarce, Miss Trey Sleuth was everywhere with reviews, websites, and blogs. Apparently Travis's was the only person in the world who hadn't read her books.

But the story he needed to know was her husband's. If there was an answer to be had, Austin would find it, even if he resorted to calling in favors from the government and the military to ferret out details.

Travis arrived uninvited at her home, but he didn't care. He parked his black Escalade beside the curb in front of her pretty duplex with the welcoming porch.

A lime-green Smart car backed down her driveway. She turned her head to check traffic, but even if he hadn't seen her, he might have known it was her car by the oversized wind-up key attached to the rear that spun while she drove. The woman had a quirky side. He'd seen that last night in her room décor. A teddy bear with glasses sat next to a bookcase reading – the lowest shelf of which contained games. Scrabble was on top and dust free. Being a strategist, he preferred chess.

Above her kitchen door, she'd painted a sign that read, *your story begins at home.*

Now, he found out she drove a kiddy car. He laughed out loud and shook his head, his anger replaced by undeniable lust.

A woman hadn't interested him in damn near forever. After his divorce, he'd refused to get involved again. Teresa was right. He could help others, or he could be married, but doing both was impossible. Saving others, particularly battered women and children, had become paramount in defining who he was.

Abused women and children did not pay Travis's fees. Corporate America and wealthy individuals paid him to do what he did best. Top rated security. Protection that wasn't available from the police or rent-a-cops. Flash the words, former SEALs in front of most CEOs and the checkbook automatically appeared.

Austin was the best tracker in the business. Finding lost items, including humans, was his specialty. But like himself, Austin's easy-going personality turned to ire when the weak were threatened.

They'd spent their childhood moving from location to location to avoid their father's wrath. In Travis's early teens, two things happened. Miracles actually. After years of stalking the family, his father was murdered. While most wouldn't regard the death of a parent as a life-saving grace, Travis had breathed a huge sigh of relief.

The second phenomenon involved his mother. While she loved her sons, she feared being alone. Over the years, she'd chosen one man after another who mistreated her. Travis and Austin protected her as best they could, but she'd believed in love at first sight – usually with some big-talking mean son-of-a-bitch. The boys ran off most men their mother brought home.

Rod Stevens was the first man who'd been kind. He'd taken their mother and her two pre-teen sons under his wing. With him, their life had approached normalcy.

As their stepfather, Rod had worked the boys, showing each of them the true meaning of being a man. Not only had they taken his last name, each had adopted his code of honor.

At sixteen, their best friend, Sam's problems at home escalated, when his step-father had beaten him in a drunken rage. Rod quietly co-opted the teen into the family and treated him like another son.

When Sam's step-father had appeared, inebriated and waving a gun Rod stood his ground, refusing to release the boy to his custody.

Travis followed Abby's car to Pill Hill, the Oregon Medical Complex. Both parked near the VA hospital. He was so screwed on this deal. Why couldn't he be panting after the busty blonde from last night's dinner? He respected other vets, and he respected the sanctity of marriage.

Abby didn't falter but walked straight to the bank of elevators. Her hips, firmly encased in form-fitting jeans and knee-high boots with spiky heels which meant her firm stride should have wobbled but didn't The hooded floral windbreaker matched her t-shirt underneath and emphasized a world-class ass previous encounters with her only suggested.

He sprinted to catch up, grabbing the elevator door before it completely closed.

"Good afternoon." He forced false cheer into his tone as he elbowed his way inside.

Her surprise was genuine. "Why are you here?"

"Curiosity."

She stepped closer to the wall to widen the distance between them. "Did you think I was lying?"

"I know you weren't." He pointed at her hand. "Even though you weren't wearing your ring."

Her gaze followed his. She studied her hand with the honking huge pear cut diamond solitaire covering her slender finger to the first joint. Her cheeks pinked as she stuffed her hand into the pocket of her windbreaker.

The elevator opened onto a long corridor. At the far end, a set of closed double metal doors bore an institutional engraved sign, "Authorized Personnel Only."

Abby had moxie. He wasn't surprised when she punched in a code, and the door swung open like she belonged. She gave a perfunctory wave to a man at a small desk whose response was to glance at his watch and make a notation on a lined tablet.

The silence in the long sterile hallway, lined with closed doors, was broken by the clicking of her heels on the tile surface. He expected her to quiz him as to why he was here. Her stride had shortened to mincing steps as she ignored the large satchel bumping against her leg.

"Can I take that?"

"No. We're here." She stopped, took a deep breath and pushed open a door.

He followed, but barely entered the crowded room. Rows of filled beds lined the walls, but this room was a gathering site. At least thirty other vets had crammed inside. Some had chairs. Some rested on crutches or were wheelchair bound. The room was packed and yet more men entered through other doors at the end of the room, crowding the area.

"You're late." A crew-cut man in a wheelchair called out. The room was waiting for this woman? She grinned, a real grin that made her eyes sparkle and her nose crinkle.

As she skirted veterans, she made her way to a bed in the corner. "What was it John Lennon used to say? 'Life is what happens while we're making other plans'."

A smattering of men laughed. She kissed the soldier in the corner bed. Unlike the others, he was unaware of her presence. A feeding tube was attached to his chest.

She leaned close and spoke softly in his ear. Many vets turned their heads, offering her an illusion of privacy while others eyed the fit of her jeans around her slender thighs. From across the room, Travis read their thoughts. He forced himself not to scowl at those lusting after her. After all, wasn't he doing the same thing?

"You're with her?" a man about halfway back asked.

Several heads twisted in his direction. His appearance was noted with betrayal in their eyes. These men had given everything for their country. Why did his presence grate?

Travis straightened and stood against the wall at military rest. "No." The relief was palpable, but an element of doubt remained, so he fabricated a story.

"Bodyguard." Hell, he looked the part. He'd done it often enough. Chins rose, and defiance blazed in a number of eyes.

"She's safe with us," a man leaning on crutches expressed what appeared to be the sentiment of the room. Several nodded.

Travis hoped his face reflected the respect he felt. "I can see that. It's the to-and-from I'm here for."

The tension eased, as the vets were appeased by his words.

"What happened?" another asked.

Travis shrugged but lowered his voice, taking the men into his confidence. "Wrong place. Wrong time. It happens to all of us."

"Amen to that, brother."

He glanced over to see Abigail fuss over the man who didn't respond.

"How long's he been like that?"

"Seven years. He came back from Iraq that way."

Travis shook his head. "Prognosis?"

"Nothing good," the man in a wheelchair next to him answered in an even lower voice.

He read the resignation of the men to the other's fate. They understood what would happen, if not this week, then one day. It was the woman they protected.

"She could have abandoned him, you know." Heads close to him bobbed. "Instead, she comes here twice a week and reads her stories."

He could see it. Everything he'd thought about her so far was proving true. Just like him, she cared for those weaker than herself. That was the reason she tried to help Pierce, the reason she was there today. But that didn't explain this crowd. There were lots of loyal spouses and families in a VA hospital.

"Why are all of you here?"

The man on crutches grinned. "We got her a microphone, so we can hear the stories, too."

"They're good."

He fought back the rush of emotion that threatened to swamp him. She read to the vets knowing her husband couldn't recognize her. Lots of people would have stayed away, protecting their hearts from sorrow and anguish. Not Abby. She found a way to give back. He might have to wait for the death of her husband, but one day, Abigail Brooks would be his.

She was ready to start. Her smile faltered slightly, but her eyes were dry and her voice strong as she asked, "Where'd we leave off?"

"They were trapped in the mining camp," a man called out.

"No. You missed Sunday. They'd escaped through the airshaft."

"That's right. They'd escaped the mines but faced an icy cold river."

"Yeah. That's it."

Abby found her place, then took the limp, lifeless

hand of her husband. Travis slipped out the door to the hallway and dialed his brother.

"I am so screwed. I think I love her," he said in lieu of a greeting.

"Not so fast, partner. Something hinky is going on. Have you seen the husband?" Austin switched on Face Time. His face filled the screen.

"He's in a coma," Travis said.

"But his face isn't bandaged or anything?"

Travis shook his head. "No. What's going on?"

Austin turned his phone to show his monitor. "According to military records, Captain James Brooks is in a hospital bed in Portland, Oregon."

Travis looked at the poorly pixilated photo.

Austin switched screens. "But Internet searches have photos that match the one you gave me. Here is the shocker, each picture is an obituary, plus he's not alone. There's a wife, dying in '05 in Indiana, another wife in '07 in Arizona, a third wife in'09 in Louisiana and '11 in Colorado."

"Same name?" Travis couldn't read the words, but with Austin's commentary it wasn't needed.

"No, changes each time, except the obituaries are identical with the exception of the names – and get this – in every case but Colorado, the wife, died with him."

"Shit." Travis groaned.

"It gets better. Guess how close each man's social security number is?"

"Identical?"

"No. Descending chronological order. And the next number up is our guy in Portland."

Sweat broke out on his forehead. This was worse than he imagined. If they didn't act quickly, Abby might well end up dead.

Austin listed his needs. "Get a decent head shot of the husband. Let's find out who's really in that bed. I'm doubting it is the man she married. And while you're hanging out, why don't you borrow his file? That might prove interesting."

"Borrow?"

"Just take a few photos."

Being the oldest, Travis had taken Rod's moral code to heart. For him, the route between points was always a straight line. Austin's path involved a more circuitous route. It made them good partners. "That guy's been a vegetable for seven years. Tell me about Abigail."

"She's smart, pretty, funny, pretty, kind, loyal and nice. Did I mention pretty?"

"I had no idea you knew that many adjectives. You've mentioned everything but sexy."

"Not a problem. Certain parts of my body could drive nails."

"You could, yeah, but will she let you anywhere near her?"

"Probably not."

"Figure out a way, 'cause I think your girl's headed for terrible trouble."

Chapter Six

"Give up," Abby spoke to her rear view mirror.
"You know the worst. Stop following me. I'm not
available."

Would Stern be waiting for her at her house?
Here were two men she never wanted to have a get-
together – the dour Agent Stern and the determined
Travis Stevens, who's black SUV hadn't veered from
her bumper. Stubborn man. She whipped the car into
her driveway and drove to her detached garage in the
rear.

Her home was an older two-story duplex with a
wide porch. Whoever said 'location, location,
location' had this house in mind. Her neighbors
boasted expensive property with large lots and
professional landscaping. While she did have a lawn
mowing service, she planted and replaced the flowers
and trimmed the shrubbery.

The other half of the garage was empty. Pierce's
Lexus was still MIA. Earlier today she offered to take
him downtown to get it, but he'd refused and pulled
the covers over his head. Choosing instead to sleep
the day away – the diametric opposite of his uncle.
Hard to believe they shared the same blood. She
entered through her back door, expecting to hear a
knock within minutes, but when it came, it wasn't on
her door but her renters.

If Pierce was still in bed, he might not answer.
Fishing keys out of her purse and grabbing his coat,
she headed out her front door, only to find an empty
porch. Her neighbor's door was ajar.

She whirled to scan the neighborhood. Nothing
on the quiet street was out of order other than Travis'

black SUV parked in front of her house. Gingerly, she nudged the door wider.

Travis was halfway up the stairs to the bedroom. He put a finger to his lips and gestured for her to follow. She searched the living area, trusting his instincts even when she didn't detect a problem. Tossing the coat across the nearest chair, she struggled out of her boots.

The hardwood floors upstairs would echo any sound. Travis may have learned to walk silently, but he hadn't done it while wearing heels. The man waited, marking her every move with an encouraging nod. The small black gun in his hands pointed toward the ceiling was an HK45 compact. She'd seen plenty of photographs during her on-line research, but this was her first experience seeing a handgun in action, making him the sexiest man she'd ever seen. Her nipples tightened as her skin shrunk two sizes.

Dammit, what did that say about her? She hadn't been attracted to a man in ten years and the one she finally chose displayed a menacing gun. This was going to require hours of therapy, because she found him exciting when she should be absolutely terrified.

She passed a tongue over her dry lips. Swallowing was next to impossible. Each step was as laborious as slogging through molasses. At the top of the stairs, Travis crouched. Abby mimicked his action.

Pierce's bedroom door stood open. The covers were tossed, but her renter wasn't visible. Sweat beaded across her upper lip. She gripped the handrail for support. If someone had leaped out from behind the banister, her shaky legs would have crumbled.

She lingered, not trusting herself to go any further. Travis moved soundlessly as he searched the second bedroom that served as Pierce's office.

Her sharp inhale of each breath was magnified. To tamp down the sound, she clamped her mouth closed.

When legs reappeared in front of her, her heart gave a happy thud that they belonged to Travis. He checked the bathroom and then Pierce's room including the closet, before curling his fingers in her direction.

She forced herself to stand and take the final two steps to the top of the stairs.

"Pierce." Travis's deep voice swirled around her, reassuring her all was not lost. "Are you here?"

A muffled noise came from under the bed. They bent and lifted the dust ruffle to see Pierce clutching his computer.

"I'm here."

"We can see that. Come out."

While Pierce crawled out, Travis's eyes twinkled. He found this funny? She had to admit there was a certain macabre humor to it, but in the future she suspected she'd be writing about Regency debutants whose job was to marry well, rather than about murder and gore. That was, if she could ever get her heart rate to return to normal.

Pierce still wore his pajamas − his dark hair stood on end. He looked fourteen rather than twenty-four.

He tossed his laptop and phone onto the bed. "Someone broke in. I hid."

"Start at the beginning," Travis said, his voice calm.

How could he be so relaxed when she was ready

to come out of her skin?

"Tell me everything."

"The doorbell rang. I ignored it. The second ring was longer, so I got up. By the time I reached the top of the stairs," he gestured toward the door of the bedroom, "the front door opened. They must have thought the house was empty. I grabbed my laptop and phone and crawled under the bed."

"What happened next?"

"Two people. One wore Harley-Davidson boots and the other black and silver sneakers. Tiny feet – made me think one of them might have been female." Pierce ran a nervous hand through his hair. His gaze darted around the room as though expecting the burglars to rematerialize.

"What were they looking for?" Travis asked, his voice gentle as if speaking to a child. It was probably the same voice he'd used with Pierce all his life.

"Don't know. No words. They spent the most time in my office but were here only ten, maybe fifteen minutes, altogether."

"Could they be the same people who ransacked Stewart's office?"

Pierce shrugged. "Yes. No. Maybe. I don't know."

Abby searched Travis's face for his reaction. His shielded expression told her nothing. She clasped her fingers together to quell her shaking hands.

"They took Stewart's computer," Travis said, "and searched your office pretty thoroughly. Why? Did you have any of his files on your computer?"

"No. Mr. Stewart's computer held most of his files."

"Most?"

Pierce blew air between teeth and turned his head so they couldn't see his eyes. "He had a jump drive on his key ring that nobody saw but him." Two high pink dots of color graced his cheeks.

Had he violated attorney-client privilege? Apparently a secret jump drive was regarded as sacred information.

Travis frowned. Abby realized her brow had furrowed as well.

"Have you called in to work?" she asked.

Pierce nodded. "I took the day off. Or maybe longer." He headed for the bathroom. "I'm going to shower and call my mother. I need to get out of town for a while."

Travis shook his head, grabbed Pierce's upper arm as he walked by, restraining him from going further. "You're the only witness to a murder. The police will insist on knowing where you are. Running isn't the answer. Stay at your mother's home until we figure out who's behind this and why. You have to remain where we can reach you easily."

Pierce sagged and sank onto the bed.

The action was over.

With nothing left for her to do, she said, "I'm going next door while you two reach an agreement." She'd almost made it to the stairs when she remembered. "Oh, your coat from last night is in the living room."

"What coat?"

"The camel-hair from your office."

Pierce followed her to the top of the stairs. "That's not my coat. It's Stewart's."

"It was hanging on your coat tree."

"The bastard liked to hang his coat in my office

because he didn't have a coat closet, but the real reason was he liked to keep tabs on me."

"Abby," Travis said. "Check the pockets. Pierce grab your laptop."

Abby dashed down the stairs with Travis on her heels. The pockets held ticket stubs, a handkerchief and heavy set of keys. She sorted through the keys until she found a jump drive shaped like a key. "Is this what they're looking for?"

"Let's find out."

Pierce placed his computer on the dining room table and slid the jump drive into the port. Travis and Abby hung over his shoulder. Pierce opened files and scanned the list of folders in each.

"Whoa. Whoa. Whoa. Whoa. What's this?" He typed quickly. "Trey, why would the man have a file on you?"

"What?" She leaned further over his shoulder. "Not one file, a dozen. Open the one that says photos. Maybe it's not me."

Dozens of photos appeared as thumbnails on a page. All Abigail. Pierce expanded them. At the grocery store, parking her car at the VA hospital and weeding the backyard.

"Organize them by date. I want to see the most recent." Travis said. Pierce pulled up the latest photo.

Abby and James appeared together in several. The most telling was a recent one of herself in a blue dress she'd purchased two months ago. It showed her sitting next to her husband, looking older than she'd ever seen him. "This isn't a real picture."

"No. It's been photoshopped for your obituary."

Abby stared at Travis unable to process his

words, but she couldn't work her way through the cotton candy in her head.

Finally, she said the only thing that occurred to her. "That's not my best side."

Travis's eyes warmed. "I know." His voice had gentled. "How did you know Stewart?"

Her temper flared. Someone was responsible for this horrid mess. It wasn't her, but neither was it the two men in front of her. She bit her tongue to keep from screaming. Pierce's boss had a photo-shopped obituary of her? In what universe did that make sense?

She didn't know Stewart. Pierce had never introduced them. She willed herself not to throw up on Travis's shoes as she forced her head to move back and forth. "I don't."

His gray eyes turned the turbulent color of the ocean on a stormy day. He rested a hand on her shoulder – whether it was to offer comfort or to keep her from falling apart she wasn't sure.

"Find a photo of him." He directed his nephew.

Pierce pulled up the law firm website photo.

She stared at the picture, dumfounded. She should have known. A sense of shock had replaced her outrage. She should have known. Why didn't she know?

Both men waited expectantly for an answer.

She pointed at the screen. "That's Agent Stern."

Travis's brow furrowed, and he narrowed his eyes to laser in on her face. "Who the hell is Agent Stern?"

Chapter Seven

Travis lived by the motto 'failure is not an option'. In the military, the success of a mission involved weaponry and strategic planning. In the private sector, he'd learned methods of persuasion that didn't involve strength, but employed a genuine desire to accomplish what needed to be done. He prided himself that he'd gotten good at it.

Abigail Brooks, however, was an immovable force. He'd laid out the facts for her, and all she had said was 'no'.

No, she wouldn't leave her home.

They know where you live. You are no longer safe here.

No, she wouldn't depend on his protection.

These people are professional killers. How will you defend yourself when they come for you?

No, they won't. They'd wanted Agent Stern.

And Pierce? Too many connections will bring them to your door. You have no idea what they're after.

No, she couldn't stay at his house.

My house is secure, safer than a hotel, and they won't be looking for you there.

No, she wouldn't leave her car behind.

Your GPS is traceable. It'll lead them to you.

No, she didn't have a plan or a clue or even a vowel.

Finally, she sagged to the couch and buried her face in her hands. Defeating her wasn't the victory he'd anticipated.

She was a strong, independent woman unlike his

mother or many of the other women he'd known who'd put up with bigger men dominating them both verbally and physically. He suspected if someone punched Abby; they had better learn to sleep with one eye open because she'd extract her revenge.

However, he also knew abuse was insidious. It didn't pounce, but slowly worked its way inside, destroying one's self-confidence and weakening her ability to fight back.

He lowered himself to the couch, prepared to gather her into his arms. She'd feel better if she cried it out. As soon as he touched her, her tousled dark head popped up defiance in her eyes. His triumph was an illusion. She acquiesced only for the short term.

"It'll take me a few minutes to pack."

"Need help?"

"No."

Any acceptance of his help was better than nothing, but he had a long way to go before he could claim victory. Even so, a giddy feeling of exhalation gripped him. Having her at his house, in his possession was a dream come true.

The wounded vet wasn't her husband. Travis didn't have to be chivalrous for a lie. He could and would seduce her. And keep her. But not before he heard her story. She had to trust him and want to be in his arms – and in his bed – preferably forever.

"Where did you meet?" Travis asked as they drove to his houseboat on the Willamette River.

Abby's fingers twisted together in her lap. The navy polish was dotted with white stars reminding him of a Van Gogh painting. Without thought she scratched her left palm. His mother used to say that was a sure sign she would come into money. He opened his mouth to tell her, but stopped when he saw her staring out the window — her gaze lost in memories.

"A New Year's Eve party." Her voice held a distant quality that had him sneaking a peek at her face. "We hadn't spoken until he pointed to a man across the room and quizzed his date, 'What's that guy's story?'"

She laughed a dry sound that lacked mirth. "His date said, 'I don't know him.' She obviously didn't play his game, but I did. I came up with an entire life for a man I'd never seen before."

Visualizing the scene was easy. Abby, with her lively imagination, would have been enticing, making other women pale by comparison. A surge of jealousy spiked through Travis. "I can see how you became a writer. Did he ask you out?"

"Weeks later." Her words were bitten off.

He suspected anger brewed just under the surface. She'd been betrayed and lied to by a man who was supposed to protect her.

Examining her history was difficult, but she soldiered onward. "We dated for a few weeks and then married."

So fast? Why?

He smoothed his brow when he wanted to rage and beat his fists on the steering wheel. He forced himself to tamp down his possessiveness. Why was he reacting now? Other women, including Teresa, had complained he'd been over-protective, but this was over the top, even for him.

With an effort he kept his voice level and calm. "Whose idea was it to marry?"

Abby tossed her hands in the air in exasperation. "He pushed me to move in with him, but I was a good Catholic girl. My parents would have known and been disappointed. I refused. But James wasn't a guy to capitulate. The next thing I knew we were in front of the Justice of the Peace getting married. Everything about him was Right Now. Immediate. He was the most exciting man I'd ever known," she harrumphed, "and in the end the scariest." Her final words were whispered.

Travis scrambled to pull her out of her funk. He wanted to park his SUV on the shoulder and take her into his arms.

Get out of your head. She'll run if you can't control yourself.

He turned the steering wheel, directing the vehicle onto the narrow road that meandered for miles in front of the river. Not the quickest way home but sitting in the vehicle was cozy, more intimate than they'd been all day. "Was he in the Army then?"

"No, he was a salesman for a farm and ranch supply, which paid pretty well. We didn't have much in the way of possessions, but he always had a wallet full of cash. Every night we partied − eating, dancing, and going to clubs. Looking back on it, now, there was an air of desperation about him like he had to cram all the good things into a very small window of time."

Abby fluffed her hair. Travis pressed his lips together, refusing to point out her unconscious preening. He understood she longed for the happier moments.

"We married two months before the World Trade Center was bombed. After 9/11, nothing was normal." Her hands dropped to her lap. "He paced and snapped at me if I said anything. He disappeared at night and refused to tell me where he'd been. We had a big fight, which ended when he told me he'd joined the Army and had to leave. He said he'd write. That was the last time I heard from him."

Travis did the math in his head. "That's over a decade ago. You didn't divorce him?"

She pressed her lips together and shook her head. He said nothing, waiting for her to elaborate.

"Every month, money was deposited into my account, so in the beginning I believed he was holed up someplace and couldn't contact me. Money was tight. A friend told me shopping at the base would save money, so I applied to the VA. They wouldn't even let me on the military facility, claiming that his social security number wasn't real."

Travis almost spoke, intent on telling her the truth, but hesitated when she continued with her story.

"The next day, I had my first visit from Agent Stern."

How was the VA involved?

"Charles Stewart?" he asked to confirm what he already knew.

She'd wrapped her arms around her chest. He turned up the heat. "Do you want a cup of coffee? I can drive through a Starbucks."

She squirmed in her seat, seeking a comfortable position. "I'm okay."

He gentled his voice. "Tell me about Agent Stern."

Her silence worried him, but as he considered another question, she spoke. "He wasn't a big man, but he held himself with such confidence. He appeared larger than he was. His suit and his shoes were expensive." She huffed out a strangled noise. "His shirt was made of some rare material that mere mortals trembled to touch."

Oh, yeah. She was a writer.

"The only thing off about him was the car. Nice, but too generic. It wasn't a car he would have driven. It lacked prestige. I figured it was a rental, which meant he wasn't local."

Scrabble. When he'd seen the game, he'd known her mind sorted details and pieced them into place. Combining that with her writing skill, she'd chosen the perfect game.

Travis nudged her, wanting to know more. "Where were you living at the time?"

"San Diego."

"Did he come to your home?"

"Apartment." For the first time since she climbed into his car, she looked at him.

Those huge chocolate eyes captured his, and for a moment he forgot where he was. The Escalade's tires rumbled onto the shoulder, breaking him out of his trance. He swerved in time, but he'd been close to running off the side of the road.

If she noticed, she gave no indication. "He showed me a badge and told me my husband had been co-opted into Special Ops. At that time, I didn't know anything about Special Forces. I didn't have a reason not to believe him. Because of his assignment I wasn't eligible for base privileges. I know that's not true now, but at the time I believed him. The weirdest thing he did was grab my chin and turn my head back and forth as he studied my face. I don't know what he thought he'd see, but whatever he found made him leave immediately without even saying good-bye. He mumbled something about how James should have provided better for me and walked out the door."

"When was this?"

"June, 2002. The next month, the money in my account doubled from two thousand to four thousand."

This time Travis didn't bother to hide his frown. Nothing about this story made sense. "With no explanation?"

"Nothing. I still don't know where the money comes from."

Travis parked the Escalade in his reserved spot at the marina. A soft ding from his cell phone told him his vehicle had triggered the surveillance cameras.

Abby's head craned as though suddenly aware of their location. "You live on a houseboat?" For the first time, her voice held an undercurrent of excitement.

His chest puffed as they gazed down upon a u-shaped pier with two rows of homes that extended over the water. "Do you like it?"

She scrambled out of the front seat and ran to the fence for a closer view. Whatever her reply, her words were lost in the wind. He grabbed her luggage from the back.

Stevens Security owned the marina and all the homes. Each was rented to family, close friends or employees. State of the art security, including face recognition software and thermal heat imaging, protected the tall chain link fence with a coded lock, preventing the unwanted from entering the ramp that led to the waterfront property. These precautions wouldn't keep out a professional, but meant most of the residents saw only invited guests.

The brothers knew who came and went. Austin's truck was two spaces over. He'd be waiting along with two other employees, the twins, Titus and Tyrone, who lived on the far side of the pier.

Abby negotiated the steep ramp in her heeled boots, gripping the rail and hugging her computer while Travis easily wheeled her bags behind him.

Water was a curative. Magical properties captured his worries and carried them away in the current. As her feet touched the pier, her shoulders eased, and the frown faded, leaving her forehead smooth.

He gestured to the left, pleased that she'd reacted the same way he did. "When did you see Agent Stern again?"

"About every six months. I was under constant surveillance but wasn't aware of it for quite a while. Almost two years after my husband left, I went to dinner with a college friend. It was nothing special, just dinner. Agent Stern arrived on my doorstep first thing the following morning, foaming at the mouth. It took me forever to convince him it wasn't a date. The next day a new BMW was delivered with the pink slip in the glove compartment. Kind of an apology, I guess."

"Did you ever see anyone other than Stern?"

Her dark hair danced in the wind. She clutched her jacket to her chest. "No, but by that time I knew, whatever was going on, wasn't on the up and up. I believed James was dead. If I didn't play along, I'd be dead, too."

"So what did you do?"

Eight houseboats were anchored to the pier, four on the right where Tyrone and Titus lived and four on the left where he and Austin lived. While each was different, none stood out as exceptional or unique. "Last house. Why didn't you talk to someone?"

"I did. The police laughed. Every time I left the house I watched my rearview mirror. I moved. I quit my job. I traded cars. I even closed my bank account."

"And?"

"Nothing. The following month money appeared in my new account just like always, except by now it was five thousand. They didn't contact me again for months."

"They?"

"The government. The government had to be behind this. Who else could control the VA and the banks?"

That gave him pause. He knew some dark corners where it could be possible. Who was her husband? And what was important about the appearance of his being married? Why was it so important that he married all over the country? Who were they trying to fool? And how did this tie into Stewart's murder?

"When did they tell you about the man in the bed?" Travis refused to call the coma victim her husband. He wasn't, and both of them knew it.

"In 2005, Stern showed up, told me my husband had been wounded and would be in a Portland VA hospital. He gave me an address. Not for the hospital, but for the house I now own. A day later, movers arrived and wordlessly packed everything. When I reached Portland, everything was unpacked and arranged. The nicest word for it was creepy, but by then I'd gotten used to 'Big Brother'."

That he could believe. Out of habit, he searched the long pier. Austin's home was next door to his. His brother lounged on his patio and gave a brief nod when Travis's gaze met his, but his attention was focused on the woman with him.

Travis knew the exact moment she realized they weren't alone. Her body tensed, and she stepped to the outer edge of the pier.

Austin smiled in a way that usually had women falling all over him. Not Abby. Another half step to the right and she'd be in the water.

"My brother," he murmured to reassure her.

Austin's blood always ran hot. Even in early November he dressed in white shorts and a blue golf shirt. The man had a core of steel, which he hid under an easy laugh and a friendly smile. Most women were drawn to him, but her face was a study in panic. She approached his brother with halting steps like one would a large snarling dog.

Austin kept his smile in place, but he'd observed her reaction. Travis hugged her tight to his side to shield her.

"Give us a minute," he said to Austin.

He headed to his house, keeping Austin in his peripheral vision. His brother relaxed and tilted his head back as though his face sought the sun amid the noonday clouds. Behind his calm features, his analytical mind would be whirling with questions.

As soon as Travis unlocked the door and dropped her bags, he crowded her against the wall. "Why does my brother worry you?"

She trembled in his arms. He'd been doing so well, holding himself in check. But as soon as he got a whiff of the enticing scent of heated woman, not touching her was impossible. His hands burrowed under her jacket and then under her shirt to touch the bare, warm skin of her rib cage.

Her entire body jumped. He hadn't worn gloves outside, and his fingers were cool. The temperature had snapped her into action.

Her hands shoved against his chest. "Why are you manhandling me?"

"Because you look like you're about to jump out of your skin. What about him made you afraid?"

"I'm not afraid." But the waver in her voice belied her words. He could have howled in triumph when she no longer insisted he remove his hands.

"I don't know." Her muscles relaxed, allowing him to mold her body to his.

He couldn't kiss her. One foolish move and everything would escalate out of control. If her story was true, she wouldn't have sex since her husband left. Anticipation tightened his chest as Travis imagined how tight she'd be.

He bent to swoop her into his arms. She gave a gasp of surprise as he carried her to the living room couch.

She half-heartedly struggled to free herself. "What are you doing?"

"Getting you comfortable. Men, employees of my company, will be arriving soon. We need their help, but I don't want you scared." He set her on the couch and knelt beside her.

While she'd talked, he'd formed an idea he didn't want to think about, but knew it was a distinct possibility. Letting go of her required a strength of will he wasn't sure he possessed at this very moment, but he did manage to rise to his feet.

Hell, he had to get away from her before he did something so foolish she'd never forgive him. He stepped back. "I'm going to make us some coffee."

Chapter Eight

Travis's house pulsed with energy, like the man himself. The houseboat was all windows and light. Dancing particles sparkled in the stream of dappled sunlight. The gray days of Oregon could be depressing, but Abby doubted this house would ever have the feeling of darkness or gloom. Travis's living room consisted of angled white couches that faced the sliding glass doors, the wooden deck, and the moving water.

Her muscles were liquid, unable to hold their shape. Everything had come crashing down on her at once. The murder of Agent Stern who turned out to be Pierce's boss and finding her obituary photo in his files had swamped her emotions and sucked her into the undertow. Normal Americans were not prepared to see laser beam red dots on their chest without at least knowing the identity of the person they'd pissed off first.

How the hell had she angered Agent Stern? He dropped by every couple of weeks. And while she'd always feared him, lately he'd been friendlier. Even so, she hadn't known whether to run screaming or relax when he regularly appeared on her doorstep.

A sharp pain in her chest made her think of a spring wound too tight. The wrong word would make her snap. Austin had simply smiled, but with that same dangerous look his brother boasted. The two of them reminded her of stalking, feral animals. She'd been prepared to jump into the cold river to avoid contact. How crazy was that?

And then there was Travis. Hot, sexy,

overbearing, insufferable Travis.

Grasping her head, she lowered it to touch her knees. She wanted drugs, not ibuprofen to deal with her pounding headache, but some sleep-inducing pharmaceutical that would allow her to wake up in another life.

"I don't have any cinnamon. Do you take anything else in your coffee?" Travis asked from the kitchen.

Hemlock probably wasn't the right answer.

"Everything." She looked at the large, somber man standing in the doorway and contrasted him with the light blue walls and white furniture. The decorations were nautical, appropriate for a houseboat, but she couldn't visualize the man, whose physical appearance screamed danger, shopping for lighthouse salt-and-pepper shakers or decorative anchors to hang on the wall.

"You're married?" He didn't act married, but what would she know about that?

"Was. Been divorced about a year, separated longer." He thrust a large hot cup of coffee in her direction along with a plate. "Made ham sandwiches. Food helps give me perspective."

Her stomach growled in response. Which he heard because a grin tweaked the corner of his mouth. "I was right."

Please. Save me from the smug, confident, totally male ego.

The coffee was perfect. The creamy, sweet warmth gave her insides a much-needed boost.

He joined her on the couch, putting distance between them.

The first bite she wasn't sure she could get down, but did. Followed by a second. Then a third. It was possibly the best sandwich she'd ever had. Not because of the ingredients but the timing.

They ate in silence.

"Another cup of coffee?" he asked as he rose to take empty plates to the kitchen.

She nodded and caught a glimpse of a woman's reflection in the sliding door. It looked just like herself, except the reflection was smiling. How odd. Despite the insane situation she was in; she felt safe here – in a way she hadn't felt for years. If Travis hadn't insisted she come home with him, she'd be pacing the floors at home, or, more likely, bouncing off the ceiling. For the first time, she wasn't under some hidden microscope. The man had a way of making her believe he could keep the world at bay. Her pulse had calmed, and her hands weren't shaking.

When the second cup of coffee arrived, she clasped her hands around the cup and prayed the heat would seep into her bones.

"Why'd you get divorced?" She'd told him her life, the least he could do is share some of his.

He didn't want to talk. She could read his bitterness on his face and waited for the brush-off. Instead, he sat and looked directly at her as though taking the internal pulse of her emotional state.

"We wanted different things. She wanted a nine-to-five husband. I was just out of the military and had started Stevens Security. She claimed I sacrificed our marriage for the business."

A Lyle Lovett lyric popped into her mind, something about, if he were the man she wanted, he wouldn't be the man he was. "How would being nine-to-five help the marriage?"

"We could eat together every night and have a social life." He grimaced slightly.

One thing for sure, Travis Stevens wasn't James Brooks. A memory of her husband's histrionic behavior at the clubs, ensuring he was the center of attention, flashed before her, reminding her that she hadn't missed her husband when he left.

"Teresa wanted us to be everything the other person needed." He laced his words with sarcasm, but underneath there was a layer of hurt that hadn't healed.

"She was young?"

His eyebrows shot up. "Yes, but that didn't excuse it. I was equally to blame. Corporate security is similar to being a SEAL. Once you're addicted to the adrenaline rush, it's hard to give it up. Austin and I looked at different fields like flame jumping, being skydiving instructors, and even mercenaries before we decided security at least had the veneer of respectability that being a soldier-of-fortune lacked. We wanted Sam to join us, but he decided one of us needed a steady paycheck. So he became a cop."

"Why did you marry?"

"Teresa was the first woman, other than my mother who needed me. I thought that's what being a husband meant."

He shook his head.

"That makes me sound callous. I expect to be responsible to my wife, but marriage is more than that. When ours failed, I had no clue how to go back and make it right. In the end, I thought she was to blame, but now I can see how I contributed."

"Did it end badly?"

A short huff of air escaped his lips. "No. I came home one day, and she was gone."

"And you didn't go after her?"

Abigail may not have had a decent marriage, but part of being a writer meant she analyzed relationships. "You didn't love her," popped out of her mouth before she had time to consider her words.

Travis sighed and rose to his feet. "I thought I did, but I suspect you're right."

The front door creaked. "Ready for company?" Austin stuck his head through the opening.

Travis said nothing, watching her for a signal.

She sucked in her breath. "We are," she said, fighting her response to his action. Never had a man, particularly a man so used to being in charge, allowed her to set the pace.

He ducked into the kitchen and grabbed the coffee pot and cups. "Fresh coffee?" he asked Austin, who was the first one in the door.

The brothers stood next to each other while Travis poured coffee in mugs. Both were tall and broad shouldered, similarly built. But it was Austin's attire that let her see how muscular they were. Travis wore long sleeves and jackets, which hid the bulk strength of his body. Abby imagined she'd applaud if she ever saw the man naked. She had no idea how wrong she'd been. A body like his was worth a ticker-tape parade.

Two black men carrying laptops joined them. Standing between the four large men made her feel tiny, feminine. Protected.

If she had brothers would she have married James? Probably. He was the first man who "got" her. He thought she was funny and bright. His abandonment taught her to see herself in the mirror, not just through his eyes.

Everyone sat. To her relief, Travis took the place next to her, not allowing anyone else to get near. Heat emanated from his skin. No cologne but the masculine scent of sea-blown rugged male was so enticing she almost squirmed closer. Much closer and she'd be in his lap.

Two large couches, an added dining room chair, and five people filled the living area. Each man needed space. Their bodies spread out, not lounged. Each spread with their knees apart. Three of them rested their elbows on their thighs and bent over the coffee table to read their laptops and tablets. Abby found herself almost squeezed into the corner of the couch.

Travis rubbed his chin. His five o'clock shadow gave his face a dark cast. "Do you remember Dewey Gilmore?"

"The sniper?" Austin asked. Travis confirmed with a brief snap of the head.

One of twins, Titus scowled. "That guy could make coffee nervous."

Travis gazed out the window at the water. "Yeah, he was a twitchy, jumpy guy who didn't look calm enough to hit anything. Yet once he had a gun and an assignment he settled. I watched him live in a tree without moving for three days waiting for his target."

A slow grin spread across Austin's face as Travis spoke. "James Brooks, Abby's real husband, has a similar personality. I think we should look at mercenaries, solders-of-fortune, and assassins."

Abby repressed a shudder. Until he listed the professions, she hadn't realized Travis and James were similar men under the skin. Of the two, she trusted Travis more, but as soon as this was over, she was so out of here.

Austin reached into his computer bag and pulled out a clipped pile of papers. "Guess where face-identification software hit on his photo?" No one hazarded an opinion. "Interpol. Not only is he an assassin, he's one of ours. Trained by Quantico. Operates under the code name – the Reaper."

Her scalp prickled and she fought to control her pulse pounding in her ears. "He has a tattoo on his lower back of a hooded man with a scythe." Her voice held the faint quality of disbelief. She'd known for years her husband had nefarious dealings, but the facts hadn't smacked her in the face until today.

Travis put his arm around her and tugged her closer, wrapping her in his warmth. "How old is he?"

"Thirty-six," Abby said at the same time, Austin spoke. "At least forty-one."

Her head spun. "He can't be that old. Who's the guy in the hospital bed?"

"The real Captain James Brooks. Travis copied his file and emailed it to me from his phone. He grew up here not far from where you're living. His parents are dead, but I've found some old yearbooks. Look at the photographs. Maybe your husband is one of his friends."

Abby reached for the books. "That's crazy."

"Oh, really? I took the idea straight from your book, *Southern Lies*."

A rock sank to the pit of her stomach. "Do you think I knew about this?"

"No," Austin's blue eyes were solemn. "Sometimes people do clever things accidentally."

Travis jerked his head between them. "How so?"

"She wrote under a different name, lived off the money they paid her and banked her royalty checks.' Austin paused as though hazarding a guess. "In a series of annuities?"

She laughed, the sound foreign in a room of intensity. "You figured it out. They must have, too."

"No. I'm sure they kept tabs on your bank account, but annuities are an insurance product and are reported differently to the IRS. Because you never deposited your book money, they assumed it was a hobby. If you'd authored your books as Abigail Brooks, your husband was in enough airports he'd have seen your name. He'd only have to read one to know how close you were to the truth. His only option would have been to eliminate you as a liability."

She pushed away from Travis and stood, gulping in air as she clung to the fireplace mantle. Her husband would have needed to kill her? Or would he have used Stern?

"Don't you think it's funny I've only had one agent, and he turned out to be a high-priced lawyer?"

Both brothers leaned forward. "What are you thinking?"

A surge of pride flashed through her. These men valued her opinion. They might have been the ones in charge, and certainly they knew more than she did, but they wanted to hear her thoughts. She thrust her shoulders back, knowing she was as tough as any heroine she'd ever invented.

"James wasn't a trusting guy. He operated with cash and owned nothing but a few changes of clothing. Yet, Agent Stern either had power with the government or over James' bank account. You think my husband knew the real James Brooks. I can see

your point, but I also think he knew Agent Stern."
She paused to let her words absorb. "Well."

She flopped back down on the couch and flipped
open the yearbook. She searched under Stewart, then
Stern, and found nothing. "What did Pierce call his
boss?"

Austin spoke, a grin spread across his face.
"Asshole."

She frowned to discourage his humor. "Other
than that. Charles something. Williams?"

"Wilhelm?" Travis offered.

"No, it was an English name that started with a
W." She flipped through each class searching last
names that began with a W. "Here it is," she said after
several minutes. "Weatherby. My husband's real
name is Jonas Weatherby."

"That sounds English to you?" Travis's eyebrows
echoed his doubt.

"What does it sound like to you?"

"An American gun manufacturer," Travis said.
"Good work, Ms. Sleuth. Now we have to find Jonas
Weatherby before he finds you."

"Why would he want to find me after all these
years? All he has to do is stop the money and have me
evicted."

None of the men spoke which gave an ugly
answer to her question. She remembered words
spoken earlier. She'd become a liability to be
eliminated.

Travis cleared his throat. "Here's what we've
gotta do. Titus, run a scan of Abby's house and car.
See if you can locate the surveillance equipment and
where the data's going. Divert it back to us. And be

quick about it. We're running out of time."

Austin keyboarded as he spoke. "I'm scrutinizing Stewart's background. Abby's money is an automatic draft from a Cayman Islands bank, but I haven't figured out the name on the account."

"We need a sneak and peek tonight," Travis said. Austin nodded. "What about the Colorado wife who didn't die?"

"Disappeared off the face of the earth. No clue as to her whereabouts." Austin snapped the folder together and closed his laptop.

Abby's anger flared. They may have seen the meeting as coming to an end, but where did it leave her?

"James married someone else?" Her gaze swept the faces of each of the men. Everyone knew this, but her?

"He's been married several times, at least four that we know," Travis said, spacing his words as though choosing each word with care. "All under different names, but the obituary photo is the same."

"The wives died each time?" Even she could hear the panic in her voice.

The brothers exchanged a look, then Travis took her hand. "Yes."

But it was Austin who gave her details. "All but one, a Nora D'Angelo in Colorado. The police thought the accident looked staged but weren't able to prove it. They believe there may have been a second person in the car when it went over the cliff, but no other body was found."

A sudden chill hit her at the core. Her heart raced, and her breaths came in shallow gasps. Inhaling deeply, she managed to regain control despite the knowledge she'd unknowingly skirted death. Her skin was cold and clammy.

The man sitting next to her hadn't listened to all her objections and let her go her own way. He'd seen the big picture more clearly than she. To protect her, he'd argued until she agreed to his way.

She owed him. Because the people who had broken into Pierce's half of her house could easily come back. This time she would be the target. Whoever said "piss me off, and I'll write you into a story" hadn't been facing death.

Travis gave her knee an encouraging squeeze. In a voice lowered for her ears only, he asked, "You okay?"

Her throat had closed, and words wouldn't come, but she forced her head to bob. He winked in response, which oddly enough lightened the burden on her heart. She attempted a smile but failed miserably.

Travis assigned jobs. "Tyrone, nose around the law firm. Find out how Pierce ended up interning under Stewart. Also, find out what Stewart keeps in his car. The police haven't impounded it, yet. While you're doing that, I have a few friends at Quantico I want to call."

The men stood at the same time as if by a prearranged signal. Titus brushed off his jeans. "Who are we expecting to show first? The murderers or the husband?"

Chapter Nine

Jonas Weatherby showered using a loofah and an expensive English gel for men. The three showerheads pounded down on his leathery hide. His back needed waxing.

It had been six months since he'd been stateside.

After that little snafu in Moscow, he'd laid low for weeks, not daring to take an international flight for fear he'd been red-listed. Instead, he traveled at night by bus, bicycle and foot over marginally paved roads and goat paths into Afghanistan. Using a purloined ID, he caught a military transport home.

There had been a time when the idleness would have gotten to him. Now, he welcomed it. He was bone-weary and would have given his left nut for some down time.

His mother's house on Martha's Vineyard offered him brief sanctuary. A sharp laugh erupted from his lips following that thought. It had been his loving mother who had sent him to live with his step-brother, Charles when her threats no longer kept Jonas in line. He'd been fifteen at the time.

She feared he would embarrass her to such an extent the congressman she was lining up as husband number four would back out of the engagement. Better to dump the son.

His east coast friends had introduced him to the world of petty theft and vandalism, but moving to the west coast changed all that. Charles showed him the lay of the land with real criminals, hidden behind a law degree and the glossy sheen of respectability.

Jonas frowned at his image in the bathroom mirror. Somewhere in the last year, he'd shed twenty pounds and his boyish look. His cheeks had hollowed out, making his face almost skeletal. Tomorrow, he'd schedule a decent haircut, a manicure, a wax and a deep tissue massage. Maybe he'd find a lively woman who'd keep him company for a while.

He shuffled through the passports and drivers' licenses, eliminating the ones he could no longer use. He liked J names. He'd been a James, John, Jason, Johan, Jeremy and for one very short period, a motorcycle-driving redneck named Jimmy Ray. The one name he hadn't been for twenty-five years was Jonas.

He contemplated retirement. With plenty of money in the bank, crawling through the mud and muck of self-destructive countries had gotten old. Moscow had been a trap. He was marked. If he stayed in the business, his life expectancy would diminish exponentially.

Charles wouldn't like it, but if Jonas agreed to deal with a few lingering details, his stepbrother would come around. After that, freedom would be his. He'd find a place to retire. He had warm memories of San Diego, but probably he'd do better in a foreign country that lacked extradition.

He stretched out on the antique bed and grabbed his Beretta. He loved the cool, sleek feel of the steel. Most guns meant nothing to him. He used them and discarded them, but the Beretta had been with him since the beginning. He'd joked it was his lucky gun, but hadn't taken it to Moscow and look what had happened.

A sharp rap on the door startled him. He sprung from the bed into a crouch, gun cocked and ready before his brain kicked in. Anybody who wanted to kill him wouldn't have knocked.

"Your mother would like to see you in the library," the stuffy major-domo announced through the closed door.

"Tell her, I'll be right down." Jonas retrieved his towel from the floor and unzipped his bag to find clean clothes.

She'd not been happy to see him. As Charles used to say "Her children were her political pawns. She had no idea how to love them."

Jonas was too old to care about maternal affection now. If she wanted to hold court in the library, he'd grace her with his presence.

The stately old mansion with its citrus and leather scents had been in the family for decades. The Congressman had loved it. It was a shame he hadn't lived to enjoy it. Two days prior to Jonas's eighteenth birthday, his stepfather had been his first kill.

His mother at eighty reminded him of the Queen of England, regal and unbending. She sat perfectly rigid on the Chippendale chair, a lace-trimmed hankie in one hand and a cup of tea on the adjacent table. He ambled toward the sideboard and filled a glass with single-malt, careful to use only three slivers of ice.

A small amount of ice brought out the peaty flavor from the smoke of the distillery, too much diluted the whiskey. The Scottish would mock him as an American. Ice was an enigma to them. Cool water would be their recommendation, but he liked the chill of ice. And they liked selling to Americans. So it was a conflict that was peacefully resolved. The rest of the world should be so lucky.

He took the adjoining chair and waited patiently for his mother to finish her inspection.

"You look much better. I'm glad to see you haven't gone to fat like your father."

He nodded to acknowledge her comment.

She dabbed her dry eyes with the hanky and spoke without inflection. "The Portland Police called. Your brother has been murdered. You'll need to represent the family."

He'd seen a multitude of reactions to murder, but his mothers was over the top in the bone-chilling department. No wonder his career had come easily to him.

He tossed back the alcohol in one long swallow and savored the burn. "I'll be leaving then."

Each time he left, he assumed he would never see her again. And yet here she sat, hale and hearty.

It was true what they said.

The good die young.

Chapter Ten

Early Thursday Morning

Moments passed in the near-darkness while Abby oriented herself. She lay on top of the duvet in Travis' guest bedroom on his houseboat. After the men had left, she hadn't been able to keep her eyes open. When Travis suggested a nap, she'd leaped at the idea. But a simple nap had turned into something more. She'd slept through dinner and into the night. The clock's numerical dial read 3:02 AM.

Moonlight filtered through the plantation shutters leaving a ladder of light across the comforter and onto the carpeted floor.

Abby rose to find a much-needed bathroom. She regretted she hadn't bothered to unpack while it was still daylight. Or even undress. The cloak of night had long been a comfortable companion. In the darkness, she worked out story lines, and on bad nights had faced down her fears. Since she'd quit her day job, her schedule had been erratic at best. If she chose to write all night long, no one was there in the morning to make her get up and start the day.

Using only moonlight to guide her, she opened the closet door to locate her suitcases to discover her clothes had been hung up. She must have been out of it to sleep while someone else unpacked her bags.

Her books, which had filled the second suitcase, lined the dresser top. Travis was probably appalled she'd brought so many for a short stay, but he didn't understand. Books were her friends. For years, they offered her security and escape when nothing else did.

She peeled off her clothes and tossed a cotton floor-length gown over her head. After twelve hours of sleep, she was awake and might as well work. She searched for an electrical socket for her laptop.

The moonlight beckoned and called her to open the shutters. Her room overlooked the pier and the long walk back to the marina.

The water, so gray in the daytime, was inky and shimmered with yellow. If this were her house, she'd string a hammock for outdoor sleeping in the summer. But it would never be her house and she was foolish to let her fantasies take her down a path she would never tread.

She opened the window to catch the scent of the water. Crisp fall air chilled her cheeks and sent a welcome shiver down her back.

Her life had changed. Stern's death had brought all the lies to the surface. No longer could she fool herself into believing her life needed to be dictated by others. Time was at hand for her to take charge.

The monthly money would stop, but Austin was correct, she had been a good steward and had enough squirreled away to carry her through an extended, rough period. If she could sell the house, she would get rid of the last thing that bound her to a life she didn't want.

Then she'd move to a place where no one knew her. Change her name. Live quietly. Travis could give her tips about security. She was thirty-three years old, young enough to start over. If she was lonely, she could get a dog, but she'd never marry again. The one lesson she learned from James was to never let one's guard down.

Movement from the far end of the pier caught her eye. She craned her neck to see two men walking toward the house. Fear jumped in her throat, but even in the dim haze few men had that roiling gate of confidence. They had to be the Steven's brothers. Earlier someone mentioned going for a sneak and peek to check out Charles Stewart's home.

Travis would have information for her.

Halfway down the stairs, she froze at the sound of the key in the lock. It was late. He'd be tired. Maybe he preferred to go to sleep and tell her in the morning. Maybe he wanted to be alone.

The door swung open. There, framed in the moonlight, stood the man who had brought her to this refuge. A shudder ran across her spine. Even this slight movement attracted his attention.

Her breath caught in her throat. His gaze took in her appearance with such rapt intensity that her heart surged and her blood pounded. She squeezed her knees together. Her breasts, which had been so glad to be free of her bra only moments before, now stood proudly at attention hoping to catch the eye of a military man.

She moistened her lips. Travis's heavily lidded gaze followed the movement of her tongue. He placed a boot on the stair. She should retreat, but her legs refused. He took another step.

The closer he came, the more her heart stutter-stomped in her chest. No way could she run, her body, every fiber of her being, longed for this. She hadn't played this game for years, but being on the shelf didn't mean she'd forgotten how.

"You're exquisite." Her knees buckled at the sound of his deep voice, and she grabbed the rail to support herself. Her heroines were never swooning-types, but the anticipation made her lightheaded.

One step below hers, he stopped, making them the same height. He was going to get the wrong idea. Actually he had the right idea, but her last shred of modesty insisted she say something besides "take me to bed."

She swallowed, hunting for her voice. "I came down to see if you learned anything at Stewart's house."

"Uh-huh." At least that's what she thought he said − his guttural growl wasn't quite a word. The knowing look in his eyes, the amused curl of this lip showed that he knew motives and her desires – all too well.

The power of his scent rendered her powerless. His long fingers touched the bow at the top of the row of buttons that ran the length of her gown. Her taut nipples ached. Twelve years was a long time.

Her knees and thighs rubbed together. If this had been a race, she would have been pushing for the finish line while he was content to move with deliberate slowness. He unfastened the top button and his finger slid under the fabric and slowly inched down to the next button.

"Your skin's glowing."

She wanted to tear her gaze from eyes that burned an unnatural silver to verify his words, but she couldn't. Cool air danced across her warm chest as he freed another button.

Hurry. Hurry. Hurry.

The warm fingers spread the bodice of her gown. His knuckles brushed the swell of her breasts and circled until he held both breasts in his hands. His calloused fingers squeezed her nipples. The rough touch combined with the warmth of his hands burned her soul. She swallowed to verify she remembered how.

Pleasure rushed through her like a tidal wave swamping her with need. A low mewing escaped her lips along with a short, labored breath.

Her eyelids fluttered shut as she gave herself over to sensation. Unable to wait another second, she flung her arms around his neck and pressed her body against his.

"Greedy, girl," he murmured as he scooped her into his arms and carried her up the stairs. He kicked open the partially closed door to his bedroom. "Is that what James taught you? To rush? Because he'd be fast?"

He was asking questions, but she had no idea what answer he wanted. She clung to his neck. He handled her effortlessly as if she were a doll. Next to him, she was delicate, feminine and enticing.

His body screamed sweaty, sensual male. Had any sexually-aware adult ever gone twelve years without sex? She hadn't realized she even missed it until this moment.

Her nightgown had disappeared. She stood naked in the middle of the room. Outside the window, water surged in tempo with the rhythm of her body. But the gentle waves couldn't hold her attention as Travis removed his jacket. Just seeing his gun increased the moisture gathering between her legs.

Calm confidence radiated off him, unlike James, who would have shoved her up against the wall in a frenzy that left her both exhilarated and unfulfilled. By the time she was close, he was done. It wouldn't be like that tonight.

She clamped her slack jaw closed. Each button on his shirt slipped through its hole with exquisite slowness. He understood an erotic strip tease. No wonder the male species of birds preened to attract a mate. This man backlit by the light of the moon was beautiful. Michelangelo's David had come alive.

She had to do something – standing still was no longer an option. Her arms hung by her side with nothing to cling to and no place to go. She wrapped them around her waist.

"No." The command broke the stillness of the room.

Who was he to tell her no? But she lowered her arms and her eyes so he wouldn't see her mutinous expression.

One finger raised her chin. "Good."

Her heart danced with joy, and she twitched to press nearer.

As though reading her mind, he stepped closer and brushed his lips against hers, pressing to gain entrance to her mouth. He deepened the kiss as she arched into him, surrendering her actions to his guiding movements.

Her hand skimmed his chest. James had been buff, but slender and chia-pet hairy. Travis wasn't sleek. A tattoo covered his heart, but the room was too dark to make out the details. Her body was round and smooth, but his muscles were delineated creating a ripple of hills and valleys. His chest was hairless, but starting at his navel a dark neat patch arrowed down, highlighting his very firm erection. Was it a roadmap for sex or was she drunk with need?

His hand brushed her thighs, his fingers sliding

into her wetness. Building. Building. *Oh, Lord.*

Her knees collapsed as she came apart. She clung to his shoulders. Her body jerked as though struck by an electrical current as wave, after rippling wave of sensation racked her.

She had climaxed, standing in the middle of the bedroom from merely a kiss and a touch.

His warm breath curled around her ear as he bared his teeth against the pulse in her throat. Had his arm not supported her weight, she'd have crumpled to the floor in a ball.

"Good," he murmured. "We've gotten that out of the way. Now we can settle down." He lifted her into his arms effortlessly and laid her gently on the bed with a strength that made her mind whirl. "I hope you're thinking about how wide you can spread your legs, sweetheart because I plan to be there a long time."

She tensed at his words as he stretched his body next to hers. She placed a forbidding hand against his chest. "This is only for tonight."

He stilled. "How about if we agree it's only for the time you're here with me."

What was that? Two nights, maybe three. Not enough time to fall in love. He wasn't her type. "Okay."

One corner of his mouth curled in pleasure. It should have pleased her and yet why did she think she just made a deal with the devil?

Chapter Eleven

Hell, no.

Travis wasn't letting her go. He would do everything in his power to make her want to stay. She was, exactly as he pictured her − in his bed. Everything in him demanded he take her fast and hard, but if her husband used that same technique, she'd lump the two men together in the forgettable category.

After twelve years, she'd be as tight as a virgin. If he hurt her, she'd shore up her defenses against him. He couldn't have that. He'd never been to bed with a woman who took such strategic planning.

Her skin left a lingering sweetness like she'd been dusted with sugar. He savored every single taste of her, nibbling at her mouth until she opened her lips and allowed him to enter. The scent of warm and willing woman filled the room, tantalizing him, upping his need to explore her more thoroughly.

He caressed her shoulders, breasts, belly and lower until she arched against him and moaned his name. Through it all, his only prayer was one of thanks and beseeching the heavens not to let him screw this up.

"Please," she begged as he slid a condom into place.

"Soon," he promised.

He wanted to take things slower, but he simply could not wait any longer to get inside her. He strummed his fingers through her fine curly hair, then inserted a finger into her very core. She wasn't as tight as he imagined, relieving his fear of hurting her.

He added a second finger before curling them upward. Her body arched. Had his weight not pinned her to the bed she might have launched herself into space.

Her excitement pushed him. Knowing he couldn't wait any longer, he readjusted his body and slid into her. Sheathed to the hilt, he stopped. Scores of women had lain beneath him this way, but none had ever felt so right.

The need to own her drove him and he pistoned into her like a zealot stalking a sinner. Still it wasn't enough.

Her nails curled into his upper arms. She was as close as he. With every ounce of control he possessed, he managed to hold back, giving her opportunity to climax a third time before he dove over the edge after her.

Chapter Twelve

Abigail's body, cuddled under his, jumped. Travis, too exhausted to open his eyes, wrapped his arm tighter around her waist.

"Travis, wake up." Her panic-laced whisper jarred his brain into action. "We're not alone."

Instantly alert, he jerked upright in bed restrained by her determined clinging to the sheets. Austin laughed − a deep throaty noise that calmed Travis's pounding heart. He snarled at his brother before flopping over into a prone position.

Austin pulled a chair to the edge of the bed and sat. "You work quick."

Travis's lips turned upward in acknowledgment of Austin's comment.

"What you are doing here?" He'd kept Abby awake until daylight streamed through the windows. And only stopped then because he feared she'd be too sore.

"Some of us have been working."

Forcing himself to pay attention, Travis rolled to his side and propped himself up.

Abby, who had pulled the covers over her head, now lowered them to her chin. With her eyes scrunched closed against the sunlight, she asked, "What did you find out?"

His brother grinned, leaned close and whispered in her ear. "I should warn you about my brother, he's not as reputable as he appears. Women find his sullen mug a challenge. You should choose me. I'm more fun."

Travis growled, but Abby giggled. The pure

sound of happiness lightened his heart.

"That's okay," she murmured sleepily. "This 'friends with benefits' arrangement is only for as long as I'm here. Then he can go back to his usual hordes of damsels in distress, and I can move on to erotic adventures with a multitude of other men."

Austin's eyes widened as his face reflected his surprise at her words. "If you're seeking a variety of experiences we can arrange a *ménage a trois*." He stroked her cheek with the back of his fingers.

Travis restrained himself from punching his brother. He didn't want Austin touching her. He didn't want any man fondling her. But her reaction told all – she flicked his arm from her face.

"Tragically, I think not." She yawned and curled to her side, shifting her position closer to Travis, who couldn't resist a triumphant grin.

"When I have a threesome," Abby muttered still half-asleep, "it's going to be with strangers."

Austin chuckled. "You've known Travis for two days and me for one. How much more of a stranger do you want?"

A brief frown crossed her face. "Someone I can kill afterwards and not feel bad about it."

Travis found his tongue. "I see, so it's not the action you feel bad about, it's the fear someone would find out." She blinked her warm brown eyes open and looked at the two men who watched her intently.

Travis allowed a small knowing smile. "I'll keep that mind." Pleased her body quivered in response.

But she was hardly down and out. "Well, if anything kinky happens, it's going into a book." Her defiant tone was in direct opposition to the restless shifting of her body. The idea turned her on.

Did she think her words were a threat? Or would

keep him away? He and Austin exchanged a look. Both agreed. Abigail Brooks had just thrown down a glove.

She bit her lips as color crept up her cheeks, which told him she'd just recognized her mistake. She scrambled for a recovery. "Let's talk downstairs. With coffee."

Did she think that would save her? That the bedroom was the only place for sex? Wait until he told her his plan for the kitchen table.

Chapter Thirteen

The shower didn't help. What had Abby been thinking, getting into a discussion of *ménage a trois* with men fully prepared to take her up on it? No matter how hard the water beat down on her, it wouldn't erase the stupidity of her comments or the tingle she felt when she considered how much the idea excited her.

Her body ached. Sex with Travis had been like nothing she'd experienced before. Never had a man devoted such attention to her. Even her toes felt cherished. Sex had always been fun, but with a certain sense of competition. He did A. She countered with B. He performed with C and she followed with D. Finally one or both would climax and that was it.

But Travis had made it clear − the pleasure had been all about her. She didn't have to act. All she had to do was enjoy. And now here she was considering not one man, but two. What was wrong with her?

That could never happen. She should be planning for her future, looking for a place where James – or Jonas, her loving husband − could never find her. Not fantasizing about what positions to try. There was a phrase for heroines who were unable to think ahead. It was TSTL - Too Stupid To Live. Miss Trey Sleuth had no intention of being a literary stereotype. This was the real life of Abigail Brooks.

She pushed her still-damp legs into jeans, found a t-shirt and struggled down the stairs, her toes sinking into the deep carpeting. The air smelled of bacon. She picked up the pace. Travis scrambled eggs while Austin toasted the bread. She stumbled to the coffee pot and poured a cup. "You can't hold any comments against a person who hasn't had coffee."

Travis made a non-committal 'um' which didn't make her feel one iota better. Austin just grinned, annoying her even more.

"So what did you learn?" Travis asked when they sat down to full plates.

Austin opened his laptop and set it to the side of his plate. "I've traced Stewart's money. He's divided it into accounts from Switzerland to the Cayman Islands. There are millions."

"Who gets it?" Abby asked, momentarily greedy. Before her common sense reminded her that of all the people he might have willed money, she wasn't on the list. Nor did she want to be.

"Don't know yet. He's never married and has no heirs I can find. I suspect Jonas will be the beneficiary. Your house," he turned to Abby, "is in your name but with reversionary rights."

She knew it. The house had only the illusion of being hers. "Which means?"

"You can use the house as a homestead and he can't take it back. But as soon as you try to sell or rent out both sides, the ownership reverts to him."

Trapped. Even in death, Agent Stern was able to make sure she remained in the role he designated.

Two deep lines appeared between Travis's eyebrows. "What else did you find out?"

Austin scratched his day-old beard. Not every man could pull off the scruffy look and still manage sexy, but he did. She compared his looks to the clean-cut Travis. When had he found the time to shave?

The two men were close to the same age, but where Austin's face appeared carefree and much younger, Travis's did not. His gray eyes were filled with ancient wisdom and secrets he would carry to his grave.

His somber concern appealed to her more than Austin's easy-going charm. Travis made her feel safe during a very dangerous situation. His brother was just another man with boyish charm and big on extravagant gestures, but Travis operated with two feet planted solidly on the ground.

"I've run through all of his local finances. He doesn't pay for any other location like a storage building. We must have missed something at his house. Let's put the twins on surveillance."

"You think we need it?"

Austin leaned across the table to snag another slice of toast. "Somebody from the family has got to be showing up soon."

Abby sat straighter. *Someone from the family would be showing up soon?* Who? "The family has been notified?"

Both men nodded. "Sam called the mother in Martha's Vineyard a couple of days ago," Austin said.

"You have her phone number?"

He turned his computer toward her. Using Travis's phone, she punched numbers starting with star-six-seven to block caller ID. Both men sat transfixed, but neither made a move to stop her.

"Good afternoon," a male voice answered. She put the phone on speaker.

"Hello?" She made her voice a little nasally. "This is the coroner's office in Portland, Oregon. We were wondering when a family member is scheduled to arrive to make necessary arrangements for the body of…. Charles Weatherby Stewart." Instead of saying the third, she added, I-I-I as though she was too stupid to know any better.

The throat on the other end of the line cleared, indicating exactly what he thought of her and the call. "Mrs. Polk's youngest son left yesterday afternoon."

His formal tone was filled with condescension, and the fact he referred to the woman as Mrs. Polk convinced Abby that the voice belonged to an employee rather than a family member.

"His name?" she asked largely to see how much information he would divulge over the phone.

"Jonas Weatherby."

"Flight number?"

"Why do you need that information?"

Wow. And she hadn't thought his tone could get any snottier.

"The coroner's office helps out-of-town family members by arranging for transportation from the airport and a hotel if they need it."

Okay, that was a big, fat obvious lie.

"Mr. Weatherby is hardly inclined to fly commercially. Your help won't be required."

He was offended she'd offered help?

"Well, okay, then."

His response was to hang up.

Travis rolled his eyes as she disconnected the call. "In that conversation you used both a New York Bronx and Minnesota accent."

"But he told us what we wanted to know."

Travis grinned. "True. It was a clever plan."

Abby clutched her knees. She had it bad if his smile made her think of sex.

"What else have you learned?" he asked Austin.

Austin lowered his head, ignoring the interplay between the two and consulted his computer screen. "I think I know why Stewart was killed."

Travis perked up. "Tell us."

"You remember the ruffle in the intelligence community about six months ago with a botched assassination attempt in Russia?"

"That no one claimed responsibility for?"

Austin nodded. "According to our friends at the CIA, Stewart is a former agent who was ousted several years ago. Mostly he's kept off the grid by doing rogue private contracting. But the Moscow job was an embarrassing mistake."

Abby waved a triangle of toast as she said, "Well that explains how the murderers looked military-issued."

Austin shook his head. "They contracted the hit."

The lines in Travis's forehead were etched deeply into his face. "To…?"

Austin' blue eyes danced with the answer and a corner of his mouth quirked up into a grin. "Who do you know on the West Coast that trains a private army?"

Travis stared at his brother in disbelief. "Black Adder?"

When Austin agreed, Travis expanded his answer for Abby's benefit. "Black Adder is a para-military operation with an extensive training facility in rural Idaho. They contract with the government in Iraq and Afghanistan, but I've never heard of them using a female operative, or in the murder-for-hire business."

"The vehicles had Idaho plates," he reminded Travis.

Travis still shook his head. "Does Sam know?"

"Yes." Austin typed several keystrokes.

"According to his computer records, Stewart kept thorough notes. Interesting... Jonas made his first kill before Quantico trained him, which has to mean that Charles coached him, and Quantico only refined the process."

"Why all the marriages?"

"Haven't figured that part out yet, but it looks like Abby was the first."

Travis picked the empty plates off the table and set them in the sink. "How often did you see Agent Stern?"

"In San Diego about once every six months, but when I moved to Portland every month, then more often."

"Was he ever out of line with you?"

"Well, he never offered a *ménage a trois*, if that's what you mean." Both men lowered their faces to hide their amusement. "In the last few months, he'd drop by for tea or surprise me at the VA. And I noticed he touched me more. Nothing overt, just friendly touches to the shoulder or arm."

"How did you react?"

"Nervous at first. Eventually, I ignored it. It was sort of like we formed a friendship. Do you think he was getting me to relax so killing me would be easier?"

"No." Travis's blank face was impossible to read. "I think he was planning on having sex with you before he killed you."

Chapter Fourteen

Abby paced the kitchen. "I'm going to get some fresh air," she announced as she opened the patio doors and stepped outside.

Austin arched a brow as he watched the woman pace the deck. "She's curious." Travis nodded absently, knowing he referred to the earlier sexual exchange.

"If we push a little she'll come around."

Travis pressed his lips together not sure he wanted to voice the opinion that he had been turning over in his mind all morning long. "I agree. Except... she's floundering. Her whole world has been shaken. With Stern dead and her husband headed this direction, I think she's struggling to figure out what form survival is going to take."

"We'll keep her safe. What's the harm in a little flirtation?"

Travis snorted. Unworldly women like Abigail Brooks would not view a threesome as a little flirtation. And much as he hated to admit it, he wasn't prepared to share. "She's an introvert who writes and has little contact with the outside world. We aren't seeing that personality. She might agree but only as research."

Austin frowned. Both brothers stared out the glass door. Abby leaned over the deck rail. The wind ruffled her short dark hair and pinkened her cheeks.

Travis spoke more to sound out his theory than to get Austin's opinion. "Since she's been here, she hasn't called anyone to tell them she's okay. Not even her parents in San Diego, but she brought twenty-seven well-read books with her. And last night at an intimate moment she called me, Tristan."

A low growl marked Austin's annoyance. "Who the hell is Tristan?"

Travis turned his back to his brother to rinse the dishes in the sink, but in truth he didn't want his brother to know how the name had unhinged him. "The man in her latest book."

"How do you know this?"

"I unpacked her. While she slept, I read her manuscript." Travis shook his head. "If she relegates me to a character in her novel – a very good novel, by the way – she'll leave when the story is done."

He could feel his brother's eyes boring into his back. "At least you got to be the hero."

Travis knew Austin's joke was meant to lighten his mood, but it fell short. "I'm not prepared to lose her."

"Your plan?"

"To persuade her to stay." He shifted his position, so his focus was on the woman leaning over the deck railing.

"Good luck. She's pretty strong-willed. How are you going to accomplish it?"

Travis grinned. Only his brother would know there was no stopping him. Failure wasn't option because a good strategist worked the angles until all the pieces fell into place. "With weapons."

Austin laughed. Abby evidently heard the noise, because she turned to peer into the house. "By holding her at gunpoint?"

"Not exactly, but as you noticed, she's curious." Travis gestured toward the front door. "I don't need an audience. It's time for you to go."

As soon as his brother was out the door, Travis unlocked his weapons closet and laid six handguns on the couch along with a taser, a stun pen, and pepper spray. His closet contained a wide variety of weaponry from C4 to flash bangs, automatic weapons to revolvers. His goal was to entice, not overwhelm.

If it were up to him, he'd take her upstairs and spend the afternoon in bed with her, but she wasn't desperate for a sexual partner. Her experience had taught her lovers were unreliable.

He slid open the door and stepped onto the deck. "Have you ever handled a gun?"

She tilted her head, her eyes almost hazel in the sunlight. The mention of a gun had them sparkling with interest. "No."

"Come inside. I pulled out a few so you can play."

He sat on the floor and gestured for her to sit between his legs with her back to his chest. He showed her how every gun worked, then loaded and unloaded each of them.

"Put your hands out with the gun between them."

"It's heavier than I would have guessed."

"Brace your elbows on your knees to give you support. Generally these are not the guns women prefer. We can get you a lighter weight one."

She did as he suggested. He wrapped his arms around her. "This model has a lot of recoil. So when you squeeze the trigger, the gun will fly back." He demonstrated forcing her arms backwards. "You need more upper body strength. I can show you some exercises that will help."

"Is it loud?"

"Yes. Next week we'll go to the target range and

shoot.

"Are you showing me this so I can kill my husband?" Her voice sounded tentative. As she turned toward him, her forehead was furrowed in a frown.

Travis spoke slowly choosing each word with care. "The man is a trained assassin. One on one against him, you will lose. Your only hope of survival is avoiding him or taking him completely by surprise."

She stiffened. "You don't think he will at least want to talk to me?"

"He hasn't needed to talk to you in twelve years. Maybe in the beginning you meant something to him, but now you're just another loose end."

As his words hit home, she sagged against him, the pistol languishing at her side. "So he walks up to me, pulls out a gun and shoots."

Travis debated telling her the truth. She wouldn't want to hear it, but she needed to know how the events would unfold.

"The chances of recognizing him are extremely rare. He'll be in disguise. You may get a sense of familiarity from someone near you, but that's a bad thing to look for, because everybody will start to look familiar and mistakes happen. I doubt if he'll shoot you. At least not up close. He will know a hundred ways to kill you and make it look like an accident, even to people standing nearby."

"So you aren't showing me this to protect myself? You're just trying to remake me into someone you'd like? A member of your team who pulls her own weight?"

He lifted her and twisted her around so that she

faced him. When he set her back down her legs straddled his. "You're a valued member of the team just the way you are. I'm doing this because I thought you would be interested as a writer."

She pressed her forehead against his and closed her eyes. "Don't make me like you. I'd rather you were a knuckle-dragging Neanderthal. Unless I'm dead, when this is over, I'm leaving."

Her solemn eyes opened, and her lips kicked upward as she searched his face. "But I do plan to use your body until I leave."

He knew what she wanted. She wanted him to laugh and make it okay, but he couldn't. This was too important. Their relationship was more than sex, and he needed her to understand that from the beginning.

His chest tightened as he hunted for the words to make her understand. "Despite what Austin told you, I'm not cavalier with my body. Cheap thrills aren't my goal. In the past men have not earned your trust, but I'd like to at least have a chance to try."

She'd shut down. He could see it in her face as she refused to acknowledge his words or even look at him, preferring to stare at the floor.

"You don't know anything about me," she mumbled as though her beliefs melted in the face of his opposition.

His chipping at the edges was beginning to yield positive results. With his finger, he lifted her chin and forced her gaze to meet his. "You are a woman who lives in her head, an introvert. Your characters are your friends and companions. You can deal with the public, but you'd prefer not to. You don't miss your husband. While you'd never admit it aloud, it has been a long time since you wanted him to return. You have a strong need to protect others. You even bought a fake diamond so the veterans at the hospital would believe the man in the coma loved you so much it made sense for you to read to them for seven years.

"You also are not cavalier with your body. Agent Stern would have had to sprout wings and fly before you would have agreed to sex with him because you didn't trust him. You keep your family and friends at a distance. You tell yourself it's because you don't want to admit your strange marital situation, but even as a child you weren't close to your parents and felt like an outsider growing up. It takes a lot for you to confide in another, even with someone you like, but when a friend needs your help, you go balls-to-the-wall for them."

She shook her head with each sentence. "You're guessing."

"Observation is a part of my job, and I'm good at it."

"I don't want to like you."

A slow smile quirked his lip. "But you do."

She reached for the lapels of his shirt. "It's a good thing you have some talent in bed because you're really annoying." And with a strong jerk, she ripped open his shirt. "To quote a country western song, what we need is a little less talk and a lot more action."

Chapter Fifteen

If a man could pinpoint the defining moment in his life, Jonas Weatherby would have chosen Moscow.

With Charles's death two things were obvious: Moscow was no accident because Taggart had set up him up. The fubar that resulted could be directly attributed to someone on the inside leaking the plan.

Men with automatic weapons laid in wait for him to arrive. Even now, he couldn't say exactly what gave them away, but some inner sense told him to run. And he had, but he'd barely taken flight before a hail of bullets rang out.

Until today, he'd never been exactly sure who "they" were. Now he knew.

Since Jonas survived, Taggart needed to send a message. By killing Charles, he hoped to ensure that Jonas would never venture out-of-line again.

He had no one to blame but himself. For twenty years he'd done Charles's bidding without question. And he'd become rich, as a result. But what good was money if you couldn't spend it? Charles lived the good life. Respectable. Stable.

In truth, Jonas hadn't wanted those things in his thirties. He'd been happy bouncing from location to location, never burdened with possessions. He wasn't the kind of man who wanted to remodel a kitchen or mow the grass. But on his fortieth birthday he'd collided with Nora D'Angelo.

Living in hotels had gotten old. Women were always abundant, but one was pretty much like another. Spend a day, a week, a month, and then move on. Nora had hit him like a speeding train.

Being with her calmed him and removed the jumpy nervousness he'd had since his teen years.

He hadn't wanted to move, but Charles had insisted. This time Jonas suggested bringing Nora. His step-brother had gone ballistic and threatened to come to Colorado.

As always Jonas capitulated and fallen back into the pattern. Marry the girl. Arrange an accident. Leave town.

There had been eight marriages in all. Six women had died who were not enemies of the state or homegrown terrorists. They were simply people who had been in the wrong place at the wrong time.

Amazingly it was the bookends who lived. Wife number one, Abigail, stayed alive because Jimmy Brooks simply would not die. Seven years in a coma. Who'd have thought it? After that, Charles insisted Jonas concoct a tragic accident, following each marriage.

But number eight had been different. Of all the women he'd known, Nora was the most like him. She kept secrets, was determined to live life on her terms and wasn't afraid to fight.

After one horrendous argument, Jonas had slept in a hotel for three days waiting for her to calm down, afraid she'd murder him in his sleep.

She was also the one woman, Charles had truly hated. She'd been in the passenger's seat when Jonas pushed the car over the cliff. Some nobody who vaguely resembled him sat behind the wheel. But as the car hurled through the air, her door opened, and her body had been flung sideways.

The pharmaceuticals in her system would have

kept her unconscious. If he were lucky, the fall would have killed her. At least he'd hoped so at the time because the resulting billowing fireball meant others would arrive too quickly for a thorough search.

Weeks afterwards, he hacked into the law enforcement computer system. Another body had not been reported. One more reason he was ready to retire. How could a man spend his life looking over his shoulder?

Secrets made a person dangerous. Nora had secrets. She was ruthless, and with three ex-military brothers, hired guns were at her disposal.

Turned out, she had loved him the least, and he missed her the most.

The trip to his brother's home was circuitous.

Trust was not part of his genetic makeup. Instead of taking the family Gulf Stream, Jonas drove through the late afternoon into the evening to Ohio, caught a commercial flight to Vancouver, BC, where he caught a train to Seattle, rented a car and drove to Portland.

He hadn't been to Charles's home since high school. They weren't the kind of family who got together to celebrate the holidays. They had devised a series of communications by which Jonas was told what to do and how to do it. They'd met occasionally. Once in Paris, twice in Madrid and spent several days together on a Russian cruise to Antarctica.

His brother spent hours harping on the importance of flying under Taggart's radar. After Nora's disappearance something changed. Tired of being the pawn, Jonas flew to DC, met with Taggart privately and demanded to be The King.

It was Taggart who sent him to Moscow.

It was Taggart who killed Charles.

It was all Jonas's fault.

He circled the block twice before parking a few streets away from Charles's Portland home. Dressed as his brother, he walked to the front door and used his key.

Inside, he waited at the window watching the street for several minutes for any sign of movement. No police cars. No suspicious repair vans. A respectable lawyer had been murdered and yet no one watched the house. Incompetence like this was why a job like his was always in demand.

Nothing in the upper levels would be of importance. Everything that mattered to his brother would be in his panic room in the basement. It had been years since Charles had shown him the room, and Jonas expected it to look exactly the same.

But he was wrong. Son of a bitch was he wrong! Every square inch of wall was covered with photos of Abigail. Jonas stared. His stomach roiled. His brother's secret life had trapped him as surely as it ensnared Jonas.

The poor sick bastard had lusted after the first woman Jonas married. All these years Charles had assured him that when Brooks died, so would she. But it was obvious the man was obsessed with her. Photo after photo showed it. She wasn't even that cute. Hell, Jonas had married more attractive women, but he remembered her as being fun. When had his brother ever valued fun?

On the desk was another photo of a young woman with bouffant hair and Abigail's face. Jonas compared the photograph to the wall for several minutes. His brother was a smart man. Surely he didn't think he could replace the woman who got away with a look alike?

Apparently he did. His brother had spent his entire adult life protecting Jonas from Taggart when it was Jonas who had needed to protect Charles from his fantasy life.

Slowly and methodically, Jonas searched his brother's computer, then emptied the safe of its contents.

In the end, he rose to study the walls cluttered with photos. It was only a question of time before Taggart discovered this room. Before leaving, he did the one last thing he could do to protect the girl of his brother's dreams. He unleashed a set of throwing knives he'd found in the closet.

Let Taggart believe his inner beast raged.

Chapter Sixteen

For the second time that day, Abby woke up curled around Travis with Austin in the bedroom. But unlike this morning the room had grown dark with the setting sun. She woke with the light from the lamp across the room.

"Do you think if you just hang out here in the bedroom, I'll eventually agree to a *ménage*?"

He grinned. "No, but if you think it's a possibility I'll give it a shot." He moved the chair to the side of the bed.

She rolled her eyes.

Travis groaned.

Abby struggled to a sitting position. "It's not. Why are you here?"

"We've got news."

Austin picked Travis's shirt off the floor and inspected the torn buttonholes. An eyebrow arched, but wisely he didn't comment.

Next to her, Travis rose, swung his feet to the edge of the bed and stood. Abby's attention was distracted from Austin's words while she stared at Travis's naked butt, sliding into jeans, commando style.

"Let's see what you've got."

She found herself pleased by the annoyed tone of his voice as he rounded the bed to sit beside her.

Austin flipped his laptop around so they could both see the screen. "Here's a snapshot Tyrone took of a man entering Stewart's home about an hour ago. Between the overcoat and the shadows it's hard to make out details. Tyrone waited, but no lights went on in the house, so he snuck around the outside to discover a slit of light from a blacked out window in one corner of the basement. I kept telling you we missed something. There's some sort of office downstairs."

Travis nodded. "We've got to check that out."

"You haven't heard the best yet. Tyrone was still in the backyard when the kitchen lit up and saw the man through the windows. Look at this picture."

Abby stared. Goosebumps rose on her arms. She could barely get the words out −"That's Agent Stern, come back to life."

"No." Travis wrapped an arm around her shoulders. "That's your husband in disguise. Look at his build. Stewart was stockier, broader across the chest."

Abby studied the photograph of the man wearing a white button down shirt with a loosened tie. "You're right. How did he manage to look exactly like his brother?"

"Neoprene, I'm guessing. He could be wearing a neoprene mask."

"He just happened to have one?"

"He traveled more than Charles. It would be a good ID for dealing with foreign banks which also tells us whose name the accounts are under," Austin said.

"Even in this weather, wouldn't it be hot and sweaty?"

"Yeah. And the fact he's still wearing it, is an indication he's not planning to spend the night."

"Pierce called. Stewart's office is having a memorial service for him. I called the Martha's Vineyard number to tell them, in case they were in touch with Weatherby, which I doubt. And Pierce called Stewart's home and left a detailed message. We don't know if Jonas will get the message or not, but if he shows up, Pierce will keep us posted as to his whereabouts."

"Is Tyrone still there?"

"Yes. I expect to hear from him if Stewart leaves."

"Why didn't James spot him? I would have thought someone like James would have been alert to others in the area."

"We thought he would be, too," Travis stroked her arm as he spoke. "And probably would have spotted a surveillance van. So, Tyrone hid in some bushes in the park across the street."

Electricity from his touch zipped along her nerves. "Wow, there's a thankless job."

Both men laughed as though they shared a joke. "We've done worse," they said in unison.

Austin's phone dinged. He glanced at the screen. "Weatherby's leaving the house now. Do we want Tyrone to follow?"

"Too risky. Have him keep watching the house. We need to check out that basement." Travis walked to the closet to get a clean shirt. As he passed the end of the bed, he grabbed his torn shirt and tossed it in the trash.

Austin closed the bedroom door behind him as he thumped down the stairs.

Since she never heard either man make a noise, the footsteps were for her benefit.

"What is your plan?" Travis asked as he bent over the bed.

"I need to work. I'm going to stay here and

write."

He gave her a light peck on the lips. "Good idea." He touched her lightly under her chin, smiled, then hurried after his brother.

Chapter Seventeen

Normally, Abby sank easily into her story, but tonight the computer monitor mocked her. Every sentence was wrong. Instead of starting back five-to-ten pages to read what she'd last written, she opened her story at page one and made changes. Tristan's blue eyes became gray. His slender build became beefier, taller, and more rugged. Just as she was about to add a brother to her plot, she stopped.

Was Travis right? Did she live vicariously through her characters? Tonight she was editing their experiences based on her new lover. Had she adapted a cloistered lifestyle out of fear, or because it truly was who she was?

When she needed sex, she wrote about it. And as her fantasies played out on the paper, they were better than real life because the hero was perfect and always said what she needed to hear. If she ever needed an erotic adventure like a *ménage*, she could satisfy her interest using the same technique.

She'd never wanted the type of man that could score gold in the sexual Olympics. Travis had some moves, but he wasn't a player. What made him hot in bed was that he was so totally focused on her. What made him perfect was that he wanted her, and he was clear about it.

He'd been right about James. She'd stopped wanting him to return before he'd even been gone a year. She hadn't missed him and truth be told, she hadn't missed other men either. When she was lonely or bored, she'd go to a writing conference and socialize with other writers.

She could keep Travis at bay by insisting she had one foot out the door. True love was a device she manufactured in her novels. Love at first sight didn't really happen. Like Santa, people wanted to believe but knew in their hearts it was a lie.

Her thirty-fourth birthday was right around the corner. She was a sensible woman. And yet a gnawing fear had developed a stranglehold. Would her heart break if she left a man she'd only met three days earlier?

Love didn't happen like this. He'd reveal the ugly side to his personality sooner or later. Then she'd see if Travis was as she suspected, another Jonas.

She opened a blank document and started a journal. Travis and Abigail, day one. The words flew across the page. This was exactly what she was supposed to be writing.

A couple of hours later, a light from the hallway illuminated the room. The sun had set without her noticing.

"I didn't hear you come in," she said, lifting her head to see Travis's body filling the doorway.

He placed the bag on the dresser and removed white cartons. "Have you eaten? I brought Chinese food."

The scent wafted through the room turning her thoughts to ginger, garlic, and chilies. She closed her laptop and watched his graceful moves as he opened the cartons and arranged the food. For a big man, his actions reminded her of a dancer - all grace, glide and strength.

"I didn't know what you liked so I got my favorites."

She sniffed the air. "Smells great. I'm starving.

Did you learn anything at Stewart's house?" She rose from the chair to peer into the contents of his collection.

He waited until she picked one and then chose another. "You're lucky he's dead."

A shiver traced her spine. Her chopsticks froze in mid-air. The snow pea fell back into the container. "Why?"

Travis shifted. She'd come to know him well enough to know he was debating between protecting her and telling her the truth. But she also understood with him the truth would win. "He was totally obsessed with you. Those photos on his computer were only a trickle of his collection. Your face is stamped on every square inch of wall space in his office."

"Eww." She placed the carton on the table unable to eat another bite. That was about the creepiest thing she could imagine. No telling where those cameras had been placed, and she couldn't bring herself to ask.

"Your husband wasn't happy about it, either." Travis put down one carton and picked up another. She caught an undercurrent of his anger and swallowed, forcing the saliva to go down her throat. Whatever he was about to say wouldn't be good.

She waited, watching him intently. He wasn't eating, but rather picking at the food before discarding it. Finally, he put his carton away. "I brought some beer. Would you like one?"

She nodded. The bottle was ice cold, but the beer didn't satisfy her thirst. Travis crossed the room, crawled on the bed and sat next to her, resting his back against the headboard.

"Did you know your husband was quite skilled with a throwing knife?"

Her stomach lurched. She loosened the corner of the beer label and peeled it back to have something to do besides stare at him. The label was real. It was safe. Travis's words were illusion, like writing - only as real as she made them. Jonas hadn't been a killer, she would have known. Wouldn't she?

But an image flashed before her eyes. Maybe there had been clues she'd ignored.

"The only thing he did that surprised me was strangling a neighborhood cat who wandered onto our balcony. I was horrified and started screaming. He told me he over-reacted because he was terrified of cats, but I didn't think the smile on his face was from fear."

Travis wrapped a strong arm around her. She curled into his body, knowing she needed to hear what he was going to say, but dreading it.

"Twelve knives were buried in photos on the walls. Each one placed exactly between your eyes. He wouldn't have reacted with that much anger had he known the photos were there. We booted up the computer and his cameras at your house and made sure they no longer feed to him."

She shrugged. "Doesn't matter. I can't go back there anyway. Too much bad stuff."

Her skin crawled. Charles had planted cameras everywhere. She needed a shower, but how did one wash away something like that?

Travis stroked her cheek with his finger. "What do you plan to do?"

"I thought I'd stay with you and see how things work out."

"That's a great plan."

When he kissed her Abby hoped she hadn't closed off all her options when the other shoe dropped, and the true Travis emerged, she wanted to be able to flee.

Chapter Eighteen

Friday

Travis' phone interrupted his dream. And it had been a good dream. He and Abby were sunbathing on a deserted beach, and he'd made progress talking her out of her bikini. Already her nipples pouted in the sun. He licked his lips, then snarled when the phone rang a second time.

He uncurled himself and stretched out an arm to grab his phone from the charging station. This had better be worth waking him up.

Caller ID displayed the words VA Hospital kicking his brain into fully alert.

He rose out of bed, grabbed his jeans from the floor and closed the door behind him as he headed down the stairs.

Abby's phone had been forwarded to his. More than likely the call was for her, and even more likely it was bad news. He thought about waking her but decided unless whoever was on the phone insisted, he would deal with this and let her sleep.

"Hello."

"Mrs. James Brooks, please."

"She's unable to come to the phone, may I help you?" When the person at the other end of the line hesitated, Travis continued, "Is this in regard to her husband?"

"Yes. It is."

"Is he dead?"

"Sir, I'm not authorized to tell you on the phone."

"Let me speak to the senior officer on duty."

"I'll have him return the call. Your name?"

"Lt. Commander Travis Armstrong Stevens, US Navy retired." Travis infused his voice with the tone of command. "Tell the senior officer or whomever you need to tell. Mrs. Brooks is going to insist on an autopsy."

"Sir, the man's been in a coma for seven years, he died peacefully in his sleep. An autopsy is hardly required."

"He did not die peacefully in his sleep and the police will want to see your surveillance video. I suggest you have the tapes ready for them. I expect them to arrive within the hour."

"Yes. Sir."

Travis disconnected the phone and opened his front door. A strong gust of wind blasted through. The patchwork sky held smatterings of blue, bordered with black as dark clouds rolled in from the east. Rain was on the way.

On his deck, Austin disassembled his patio furniture and was stacking it to store for the winter. "This storm is going to be bad. I can feel it in my bones," he said when Travis stepped outside.

He lifted the stack Austin finished and carried it to the storage building. "Weatherby's made his first hit."

Austin looked up screwdriver in hand. "Who?"

"The husband."

"Did you insist on an autopsy?"

"Yes. I'm calling Sam right now."

"Get dressed. We need to meet him there."
Austin lifted his chin and studied his brother's face.
"Bring Abby."

Travis struggled with the need to argue, but Austin was correct. His bigger fear was leaving her alone. Underestimating the man she called her husband would be a mistake.

He took the stairs two at a time. She was awake, judging by the sound of the shower. He dropped his jeans on the bed. Abby gave a squeak of surprise as the shower door slid open.

"We need to hurry," he said, stepping inside without asking for permission. He pulled her to him, his arms around her waist and nestled close, sorry that the few hours of respite were ending.

Whispering in her ear, he told her about the call.

Her body tensed, making her movements wooden.

She was resilient. She'd bounce back. Sure enough, he'd barely released her when she slid the door open and stepped out. Steam covered the mirror, preventing him from seeing her face.

He finished showering and wrapped his still damp body in a towel. In the bedroom, Abby sat naked on the edge of the bed, her gaze vacant.

"Are you okay?"

"Sometimes…" Her voice was distant as though speaking from a place deep inside her. "When we make love …. There is a surreal quality to our lovemaking that takes me out of the equation. Like I'm living in a book come to life… But death? Maybe this is a book I need to put down.

She wanted to bury her head in the sand. He understood that. So many people turned their face from unpleasantness, refusing to see problems. But she no longer had that option.

To get her mind on other things, he asked, "Do you know anything about the man's family?"

"Not really." She rose, reached for a pair of panties and slid them up her thighs. He stopped rubbing the towel on his chest, spellbound by her action. "I googled him last night, but I didn't find anything of interest."

She pulled black slacks over her silky legs, then tossed on a plain black t-shirt. Travis was a little disappointed that she chose her ninja-girl outfit. His stomach unknotted when she slipped her feet into leopard-print shoes with a high heel. She stared at her image in the mirror.

Travis stood ready at the door when she disappeared back into the closet. When she emerged, she wore a cream-colored sparkly shirt under a long black jacket.

He opened the door only to have her re-enter the closet. "You look," he started to say 'fine' but changed to, "appropriate."

"I don't think so, but I hate everything I own today, so I'm not sure changing will help."

"You're beautiful."

The sorrow in her eyes lifted. She didn't smile, but she was at least ready to leave the bedroom.

Chapter Nineteen

The morgue was packed wall-to-wall with police. It was suffocating, and the heat, the bright lights, and the antiseptic odor nauseated Abby. She looked around wildly searching for the exit.

Sam's partner, Grant, must've seen her distress because he came forward to guide her out of the room. "There's no reason for you to see this."

Travis and Austin fit in with the cop shop guys. She grabbed a nearby elevator and zipped to the top – James's floor. The door opened onto an empty, silent hallway. Even the security desk was deserted. No doubt everyone was in the morgue determining why the police insisted on an autopsy for a man who had spent the past seven years in a coma. She panted, not from exertion, but from the thick airless atmosphere.

Several of the men ensconced in neighboring beds diverted their attention to her as she came through the door, but most turned their heads not wanting to acknowledge her pain. There was nothing left to do but say goodbye. And yet acknowledging a bed stripped to the mattress didn't satisfy her inner anxieties. Her life was a hollow, brittle sham.

Swamped by sorrow, she pulled several books from her shoulder bag and placed them on James's bed before turning to the men.

"Please see that whoever wants these gets them."

Most nodded, one managed to say thanks before Abby was overcome with unexpected emotion and spun away to hurry out of the room. In the hallway, she gulped deep breaths and fought back tears before steadying herself and trudging to the elevators. Each step required her brain to insist on the next step forward. She glanced at her heels to make sure they hadn't morphed into concrete blocks.

She didn't want to be here. Returning to the morgue would shatter the fragile control she had over her emotions. Except for the brief marriage, she'd been alone all her life, but never lonely. Today she stood isolated from the world.

The elevator door opened, and Travis exited. He'd come to find her. Relief swept over her as she gazed into his concerned and sorrowful eyes.

He gave her a lopsided grin that made her heart sing and lightened her worries. "Here you are."

He must have sensed her mood because he wrapped his arms around her and drew her close. His hug forced her brain's panicked fears to evaporate.

He was right. Here she was.

In a hospital, she hoped she'd never visit again. Seven years of her life had been spent here, and for what? A charade with no particular purpose. Why had she been unable to extricate herself from this Kafkaesque novel?

Being near Travis was always intense, but something internal burned within him today. He was alert. He was ready. He loved this aspect of the job while she wanted to climb back into bed and pull the covers over her head.

That thought stopped her. Retreating was the old Abby. Now, new and improved, she faced the things that went bump in the night. While it might scare her, the man standing next to her would help her get through it.

"The security cameras didn't pick up

Weatherby."

He used a soundless voice. If she hadn't been standing next to him, she wouldn't have been sure he was speaking. The low timbre was calm and would have been soothing had every nerve in her body not been standing on end.

"Did he hack into their security?"

"No. Figuring no one would care about a man in a seven-year coma, they didn't bother."

Goosebumps rose on her skin. "They?"

"Check this out." Travis played a video clip on his cell phone.

A woman dressed in a nurse's scrubs walked the hospital corridor, her sandy blonde hair bound in a bun at her nape. She pushed open the door to James's room. Abby noted she favored her right leg. "That's the woman who set up Agent Stern."

Travis nodded. "Good eye. Your ability to see details is an asset. Here's the second tape."

The praise warmed her heart and spread outward to her skin. She watched the woman bend over James's bed. From the pocket of her scrubs, she removed a syringe. The camera angle hid her actions, but whatever she did was effective, because he was dead now. The woman exited the room as quietly as she entered.

The elevator opened, and a small group of doctors exited. Neither Abby nor Travis spoke until the men were out of hearing range. Two deep vertical lines separated his eyebrows.

"Austin is running facial recognition software to confirm our suspicions."

This tape should have confirmed what he and Austin believed. Why was he unhappy? "What?"

"We're missing something big."

Abby pieced together the information he'd given her. Travis and Austin expected her husband to be the one coming after her, but instead the girl who arranged for Agent Sterns's death showed up. What did that mean?

"Could they be working together?"

"Who?"

"My husband." Funny, that she had trouble with his name. Was he still James or was he Jonas? Or was he a man so fragmented by his many identities even he didn't know who he was?

"Could my husband be working with Charles's killers? Remember what Pierce said. The girl said Jonas sent the birthday gift. Did he have a quirk in his personality that would send a hooker to kill his brother?"

"A professional assassin would never trust another person to make a hit, particularly not an important one. If he orchestrated this, he might have hired the girl for a distraction, but he would have done the deed himself. And thanks to your video in the garage we know that's not true."

Austin arrived on the next elevator. His face wore the same hyper-intense expression as his brother. "Ready?"

Travis nodded. "Let's go." He gestured toward the door to let Abby go first.

"Where are we going?" she asked.

"Our office."

"You have an office? I thought you worked out of your house."

"No. That's been for your benefit, so you wouldn't be as easy to find."

Chapter Twenty

Stevens Security was located on the fifteen floor of the International Plaza. Prestige came with a price tag. The exclusive address had aided them in building the company to the point it was bursting at the seams in just four years.

In addition to the brothers and the twins, they employed a bookkeeper, a receptionist and two transcribers who took the agents' notes from the field and created document files. In a matter of weeks, they were moving to a larger space seven floors higher in the building.

As Travis escorted Abby to the door, his pulse quickened. Would she be impressed?

He eased the scowl that cramped his face. What the hell was he thinking? What difference did it make whether or not she was impressed? CEOs of major companies had visited his office, and while the space was designed to put people at ease, the use of expensive materials and technology screamed Stevens' Security was a major player. So why worry if the easy-going woman by his side would like it?

Was he like the penguins he'd seen on a recent television show, building a nest to attract a mate, so the female would choose him because he could provide for her? Never had he behaved in such a primal fashion. He hated to admit he saw the advantage of clubbing a woman over the head and dragging her home. It'd be a lot easier.

When her eyes lit up, he questioned why he'd worried. Hell, up until a few minutes ago, Abby had thought he worked out of his house. His office had to be a step up. Quickly he introduced her around the office and gave her a brief tour.

When they reached his office, he said, "Austin and I are going to work on the computers in his office. Use my desk, my computer. Whatever you need."

"I have my laptop with me, so I'm set. Can I get your Wi-Fi key?"

"Not a problem." He got her settled before joining his brother across the hall.

Austin had already booted up a bank of monitors and was pouring over laborious columns of figures. Travis pulled up a chair beside him.

"Is she going to be okay?" Austin's tone was filled with concern.

"Yeah." What was his brother seeing, he wasn't? "Why?"

"Because if they've eliminated a man in a coma, who could cause no harm that has to mean Abby has to be next on their hit parade. How's she going to react when someone pounces?"

"She's calm under fire. You should have seen her the night Stewart was killed."

Austin shrugged. "She thought she was rescuing Pierce, not the target herself. Stick close to her."

"Exactly my plan."

His brother snorted. "Black Adder shouldn't have known about the real Captain James Brooks, much less cared if he were dead or alive."

"Unless they thought he was the real Brooks."

"Whoa. That'd be really bad information. We need to look for another player in the equation," Austin said. "But who?"

"What if Stewart wasn't as separated from the

government as we've been told?"

"How are we going to find that out?"

"Follow the money."

Before Austin could respond, a loud shriek came from across the hall. Both he and Austin leaped out of their chairs. Travis's crashed to the floor as he pulled his gun from his shoulder holster and ran flat out.

Abby stood behind his desk, staring at her laptop as though it had transformed into a serpent and was coiled to strike while she pushed buttons on her cell phone.

"What?"

"My publishing house has dropped me."

Travis took a deep breath and tried to slow his heart rate as he stepped forward to offer her a comforting hug. "That's all?"

She swirled on a heel, ducking out of his embrace and backed to the window. "That's all?" Her voice rose an octave, and her open palm smacked the glass hard enough that the sound echoed in the room. "That's major."

Wrong way to approach her career. He started to speak, but she held up her hand to stop whatever comment he was about to make. Austin murmured something as he passed. Travis missed his exact words but gleaned the essential message that mocked his earlier statement Abby was calm under fire.

"I got your email," she said, into her phone.

Travis looked past her shoulder at the email from a literary agency and let his tense muscles relax.

"What did my editor say? My sales numbers are good." She pushed the button to put the call on speaker.

"They're great. But not only are they not publishing your next book, they're declining to publish anything of yours ever again."

"Why?"

"No one knows. The word came down from on-high and is not up for discussion. Do you want me to start marketing it to other houses?"

"Give me a minute." Abby pushed the mute button. "What do you think?"

Both men shook their heads as Travis said, "we need to locate the source first. Otherwise, if this continues to happen, it could doom your career. In the meantime, act normal. Pretend you're upset."

"Pretend?" she snapped.

She glared at him, then punched the mute button. "Let me finish the book, then we'll discuss it."

"Okay, honey, I'm so sorry."

"I'll keep you posted." As she hung up, she whirled to face the two men. "Who has that kind of power?"

Travis wanted to hold her and tell her everything would be okay, but he couldn't promise a lie. The best he could say was, "That's exactly what we're trying to find out."

Chapter Twenty-One

Pierce wiped his sweaty palm across the leg of his pants as he crossed the crowded lobby to give his condolences to the senior partners. His tie strangled him. His shoes pinched. Somewhere in the crowded room, one of his uncles' employees was present to make sure nothing happened to him, which was supposed to make him feel better.

It didn't.

He didn't want to be here and would have refused altogether had Trey not needed him.

"Pierce," a group of interns clustered around a tub of iced beer called to him. One of them lifted a bottle in an invitation to join them. He veered in their direction. A cold beer would settle his stomach.

"Heard you were here the night it happened."

Pierce nodded as he put the proffered bottle to his lips and took a large gulp.

"You didn't hear anything?"

He choked on his first swallow. Someone thumped his back. "I heard a woman calling his name in the hallway," he gasped, "but she sounded like a party girl."

He glanced at the two female interns. Neither one was particularly pretty. Both wore identical scowls at his reference.

"No offense," he apologized automatically. "At the very least she sounded intoxicated."

"You didn't check?" the taller blonde asked. Pierce racked his brain to remember her name, but came up empty. It didn't matter. Who was she to question him?

"I was in the middle of *Watson v. Ellis,* which Stewart demanded be on his desk the next morning."

He leaned against the bookcase and took another long swallow, managing not to choke this time.

"Have you heard what's going to happen with your intern position?"

Pierce stared at the short, brunette woman who spoke. It hadn't occurred to him he might lose his job. The beer churning in his stomach turned sour.

"Why? What have you heard?"

She shook her head but glanced at the others. All gazes connected, exchanging hidden messages and then gave him looks of pity intermixed with a competitive glee. Aloud they'd moan about his fate, but secretly they were overjoyed there was one less candidate for the few permanent positions within the firm. His job was history. Nine months of slaving away for nothing.

"Gotta go pay my respects." He pushed away from the bookcase, leaving his partially finished bottle on the table. If he was going to be fired, why the hell was he here?

Gritting his teeth, he traversed the crowd, slowly making his way to the floor-to-ceiling windows that served as a backdrop for the nine senior partners.

"Pierce, my boy," Mr. Stanton greeted him. "We've been looking for you."

Pierce bared his lips to show teeth and hoped they took it for a smile.

"Mr. Weatherby is here to collect Charles's personal items which are in a box by the front door. " He pointed.

Pierce forced his attention away from the slender man with the cruel face standing next to the senior partner, unable to believe this was Trey's husband.

"You want me to carry a box?"

The men laughed as though Pierce had been purposely funny. "No. He needs you to show him which car belongs to Charles. You can do that, can't you?"

Pierce's lips moved, saying, "Of course." But his brain worked hard to find an excuse not to be alone in the dark parking garage with Mr. Stewart's brother. *Where was Travis's man?*

"Now?"

"Now."

Seeing no way out, Pierce forced his feet to move, but all he could manage was a shuffle toward the door.

Jonas Weatherby dropped into step beside him preventing him from searching the room for someone who could help. "Are you okay?"

"No. I've been sick."

The open box of personal possessions was half-empty. Charles Stewart hadn't been the kind to bring in family photos. Two large framed diplomas from Harvard rested against the wall.

The brother pursed his lips in disgust "I'm sure there's a wall somewhere in this office where those can find a home."

Lifting the box, he handed it to Pierce.

Loathing welled like bile from his belly. The box wasn't heavy, but this odious man treated him as his lackey. While Pierce fumed internally, the other man punched the elevator button, stepped aboard and pushed the P1 button. Pierce reluctantly followed him inside.

"Sorry to hear you haven't felt well. It's hard to watch someone die."

Goosebumps raised on Pierce's arms and the air

chilled.

Was this his end? How did Weatherby know that he'd had bugged Stewart's office?

Gripping the box with fervor, he wondered how to get out of this trapped space.

When the door opened, no matter the floor, he'd drop the box and make a run for it.

Jonas produced a key from his pocket and placed it in the keyhole. The elevator came to a halt. "Where's Abigail?"

Pierce found himself looking at the business end of a nasty-looking gun. His first instinct was to play dumb, but the cool, calmness of the other man's face convinced him that might be a fatal error. When his uncles were angry, they got quiet. He suspected this man might have the same emotional response.

"I don't know."

The gunman cocked his head. A small cruel smile tilted his lips. Pierce swore as he silently evaluated his chances of survival. His brain hummed in overdrive. Plans to escape came and went with the speed of light.

This man planned to be judge, jury and executioner.

Jury.

He'd spent three years in law school. The one thing he'd been trained to do was argue a case. And Charles Stewart had taught him one important factor – conventional wisdom never won the day. There was always another scenario to be played out.

"You're lying."

The cool dulcet tones sent a shiver down Pierce's back. He didn't doubt for a minute that this man was a professional killer.

Winners wrote history. Stewart had drummed that into him. Think. What was his younger brother not expecting?

"I might be able to reach her by phone."

The cold eyes narrowed and his forehead furrowed. Just as quickly his features smoothed. Weatherby and Stewart shared certain traits. Both thought quickly. Both made snap decisions. Pierce had spent nine months learning to circumvent Stewart. Hopefully, that training would come to good use today.

"So call her."

"Sometimes I lose service in this elevator." Pierce hesitated before pulling his phone from his pocket. When Weatherby didn't appear fazed, Pierce propped the box on his knee, pulled out his phone and hit Favorites. Travis's number was the first one. He pushed the screen.

"Speakerphone," Weatherby commanded.

Pierce obediently obliged.

"Travis," the voice barked out.

"I'm in an elevator with Jonas Weatherby. He would like to speak to Tre – uh –Abigail."

The phone was silent for a brief moment before Travis responded, "Just a moment, I'll get her."

His uncle's calm voice eased the tightness in Pierce's chest.

Weatherby took the phone from his hand, and Pierce stepped further into the corner wishing he could disappear. The ceiling, which was at least twelve feet from the floor, had a small rectangular door, but he wouldn't be able to reach it in time to escape.

"Hello." Abby's voice held a slight tremble as it

came through the phone. The elevator was silent. Weatherby must have taken the phone off speaker. Pierce sank to the floor still holding the open cardboard box. The nameplate starred back at him. Charles Weatherby Stewart, III. A name he hated.

"Abigail."

Pierce looked up when the other man spoke. The earnest tone surprised him. He spoke the woman's name like a caress. Pierce had expected a slick, taunting note, followed by a macabre laugh and the words, "*Pierce is going to die.*"

"I need to see you, kitten."

Abby's anger came through like a police siren, high and piercing. He couldn't make out the words but the tone was definite.

"Shut up a minute and listen."

Fear clutched Pierce's throat. He wanted to snatch the telephone from the killer's hand and beg his landlady to not rile him.

"Pierce is fine."

Right now. But if she kept it up, he might not be.

"It isn't my intention to hurt him, or you either. But we need to talk. Besides, I have some things for you. Meet me at your house in fifteen minutes. Bring a bodyguard, if you'll feel safer." He clicked the phone off before she could answer.

Pierce scrambled to his feet. If he encouraged her to bring Travis, he probably didn't want to kill him. The elevator started its descent. "Do you have keys to Mr. Stewart's car?"

"No. Do you?"

"At home."

"Well, I don't suggest driving it. It's probably

rigged with explosives."

Pierce fixed the guy with a steady stare. "I don't understand. Are you the good guy or the bad guy?"

"I think it depends on your perspective, but in regard to Abigail, I'll be the man who saves her."

Pierce bit his inner cheek to keep from hooting with laughter as he considered Travis's reaction to that statement.

Chapter Twenty-Two

Travis and Austin opened the deep supply closet and armed themselves.

Curious, Abby craned her neck to see inside. She couldn't identify most of the items lining the shelves. "How many weapons do you own?"

Austin shrugged as he exchanged the belt he wore for another seemingly innocent-looking belt that she bet was anything but. Travis toed off his shoes and pulled on another pair.

When both men stepped away from the cabinet, she inched forward and peered inside. Guns, both big and small, hung on the walls. Shelves covered with tasers, ammunition, and golf-ball sized black things were crowded together. Vests hung on hangers. She scanned the array of weapons lined up in the cabinet. A gun would ruin the line of her pants. But she could slide a stun pen in her jacket pocket, and no one would be the wiser.

"Mind if I take a stun pen?"

"Good idea." Travis eyed her clothes. "Take two. One for each pocket."

She took another and slid it into the opposite pocket. Fully armed, a warm glow flowed through her as she visualized herself wearing double six-shooters in an ancient Western movie. "Take that." She whipped the pens out of her pocket in a showdown move.

Out of the corner of her vision, she caught Travis's grin.

"Ready?" Austin asked as he locked the supply cabinet.

Travis's expression sobered. "We'll see you there." He took her arm to steer her toward the door.

"We're taking two vehicles?"

"Yeah." He pushed the elevator button, then wrapped an arm around her waist and tugged her to him for a quick kiss. "Plus Tyrone and Titus are already on their way as backup."

Both men seemed buoyant, calm and poised. When Travis had confessed he was an adrenaline junkie, this was what he'd meant. While she dreaded the confrontation, he loved it.

"Do not allow him to get you alone."

Was he kidding? She didn't need that advice. No way would she allow her long-lost husband, turned assassin, to get her alone. Of all her flaws, she didn't possess a death wish.

# # #

Travis lacked his usual confidence. Nothing about this situation was going according to plan. What was so important that Weatherby needed to talk to Abby? And why the hell did he encourage her to bring someone along for protection?

If he wasn't pulling the strings, and Stewart was dead, who paid Black Adder? And when had Black Adder, a bastion of male operatives, started using a female?

Nothing added up. Austin hadn't enough time to trace funds. A surge of guilt spiked Travis's gut. They hadn't called Sam. With an international criminal, he would not only want control, but he'd insist Weatherby be taken alive and that they arrest him, which might not be in Abby's best interest.

But Sam was family, Travis called him as they pulled out of the parking garage only to discover Austin had beat him to it but mere minutes.

Travis parked the Escalade deep in her driveway as close to the rear door as possible. The dark house appeared empty, but that was a façade. His skin prickled as he remained alert for an ambush and hoped Tyrone and Titus were hidden nearby, doing the same.

The rear door had opened a crack before he and Abby reached it. As they stepped on the deck, a deep jovial voice called out, "Welcome home."

Abby stiffened.

"Breathe," Travis kept his voice low and soothing.

Her gaze met his and a weak grin crossed her face. "Here goes nothing."

"I've got your back," he said to give her confidence and prayed it was true.

Enough afternoon daylight streamed through the windows to lighten the room. Pierce sat at the wooden kitchen table. His skin lacked color, but he didn't appear injured.

Her husband leaned against the sink, a 9mm sub-compact Beretta in his hand.

Jonas's face bore the look of a seasoned warrior. He might have had eight to ten years on Travis, but his body was tight and fit. How had Abby not known this man for what he was, even twelve years ago?

"I'd suggest we disarm," Weatherby's casual tone conveyed the message that he recognized Travis for the trained combatant he was and wasn't worried. "But you and I both know it wouldn't matter."

No, it wouldn't. Both had a thousand ways to kill at their disposal. He had no problem defending his life, Pierce's or Abby's, but the violence might spell the end of his relationship with her.

This was who he was. Better she know now than be surprised later.

Jonas didn't twitch, but he didn't stand in one place either. He shifted his stance, pacing from behind the table to the sink and then back. His attention riveted to his wife.

"Kitten," his voice was almost a croon. "It's good to see you. Did you miss me?"

Abby sucked in her upper lip as a quizzical expression crossed her face. She hadn't seen her husband for twelve years. Travis saw her shock, whether it was due to his physical change or the sheer bafflement of how she'd ever hooked up with him in the first place was unclear.

"Did you think I would?" Anger tinged her tone but not to the point it ruled her.

Travis was pleased she stayed in control. "Or did you think after the first decade had passed, I'd still be burning a candle in the window for you because you sent money every month?"

Laughter lit Jonas' eyes. "I'd forgotten your vivid imagination. But let's get a few things straight. The money, cars, and houses weren't from me. That was Charles' doing. He never figured the real James Brooks would last as long as he did in a coma. Once he was dead, Charles planned to marry you. For real. Not our little sham of an adventure." His tone mocked her twelve years of living in suspended animation waiting for a man who didn't care.

Travis willed his body to stillness. More than anything, he would enjoy planting his fist in Weatherby's face.

Abby's features looked stricken by his words, but pride overcame her hurt and anger. "What makes you think I would have married your brother?"

"Step-brother, please." His face morphed into displeasure. "Charles could be very persuasive. He always kept something in reserve that gave him the upper hand. Who knows what he had or why he chose you, but I think you reminded him of someone from his past."

Jonas's casual shrug indicated the answer didn't concern him. Travis considered the knives he'd found in her photos and doubted the other man's words.

"Who wanted him dead?" Abby asked, proving that being a mystery writer came instinctively.

Jonas snorted. "Who didn't? But I didn't come here to discuss that." He pulled a briefcase from under the table. "I cleaned out his home safe. You get the cash. He would have wanted it that way."

With two sharp clips, he unlatched the locks and lifted the lid. He turned the case so she could see the interior filled with neat stacks of bills.

At the sight of the money, Pierce gave a sharp inhale Travis heard across the room. Abby stepped closer to the table, her focus on the case.

"How much?"

"Didn't count it, but I'm guessing around one-hundred—fifty K, more or less."

Her head moved from side-to-side in disbelief. "Who keeps that kind of money in a safe at home?" No one answered her question. "What am I thinking? Someone who deals with illegal stuff would need a lot of cash around. Or is this money counterfeit? Is that why I'm getting it?"

Jonas ignored her questions and lifted the shade on the glass door to survey the yard. "Consider it a going-away gift. You're no longer safe here. Take this money. Disappear. In the pouch above the money, there's a passport and a driver's license to get you away from here, as well as the deed to this house. Don't put the house on the market. Wait a year or two. Otherwise, they will be able to find you."

"I can't just pick up and leave."

Travis willed his face to impassive, but he longed to reassure her she would be safe around him. She must have known what he thought because she spared a quick, reassuring smile when she looked his direction.

Jonas had lost focus. His duty, as he saw it, must have been complete because he turned his attention to leaving. He stared out the window when he said, "Then stay here and die, if you must. I did the best I could for you for Charles's sake."

Travis seriously doubted that was true. He'd kept purposely quiet, but now was his opening. "How high up in the CIA does this go?"

Jonas pulled back and let the drape fall into place. Once again, he took Travis's measure in a lingering glance before he answered. "Higher than you would want to believe. If you care for her," he nodded in Abby's direction, "persuade her to leave."

"Where are you going?" she asked.

"Somewhere safe. Take care."

Before he could turn the doorknob and be gone forever, Abby said, "Wait. Why did you marry me?"

For the first time, he appeared sincere as a sad smile curled his lips. "True love, kitten." He puckered his lips and tossed her a kiss as he disappeared out the door.

Travis leaped into action. "Pierce, where's his car?"

"A couple of blocks away by the park."

"Did you get that?" He asked Austin.

Abby slid her hand into the pocket of the briefcase and pulled out the paperwork Jonas had said would be there. "Who're you talking to?"

"The team. Stay here, I'll be back."

Chapter Twenty-Three

The tension in Pierce's face dissipated when the door closed behind Travis. "Lock it," he whispered.

Abby shook her head. "Travis is coming back."

He rose from his chair. "I'm moving, the sooner, the better, I think. This whole situation cost me my job."

"I'm sorry."

"Don't be. You've been a great friend. I probably wouldn't have gotten that position if it hadn't been for you." He sighed. "I wanted a safe place in corporate law. Now I see there is no protecting yourself. The guy in the back room is always the victim. No wonder my uncles think they're the ones in charge."

Within minutes of the door closing, an explosion shook the ground and rattled the windows. Abby had never heard a bomb before but nothing else could have been as loud. Her heart contracted painfully. Travis was out there. Was he okay?

Her first instinct was to run to him, but caution had her creeping to the window. The narrow view of her yard told her nothing. She bolted up the stairs, taking them two at a time, where she could see a portion of the park.

A black cloud billowed into the sky. Other than that, nothing was visible. She heard the rear door close. A faint voice called, "Abigail."

She thundered down the stairs and dashed through the living room to the kitchen.

A smear of blood ran across the floor from the door toward the sink. Sprawled across the tile was the crumpled body of the man she had married.

"James." The old name came to her lips easily even as if it was a lie. Dropping to kneel at his side, she lifted his head into her lap. A worn leather satchel was propped against the cabinets.

She dug for her phone only to realize she hadn't carried it with her for several days. "I've got to call an ambulance."

He gripped her arm with more power than she would have imagined. "No." His breath ratcheted from deep in his chest. Blood pooled on the black and white tiles. His crisp suit was torn and bloody.

"They're close," he whispered. She leaned her ear closer to his mouth. "My car. Remote control. Explosion threw me into the bushes. They have to make sure I'm dead. Taggart doesn't accept failure."

"Who's Taggart?"

Pierce burst through the door, banging it against the wall.

"Call 911," she said.

Pierce produced a phone from his pocket but didn't dial. "I think it's too late."

Abby looked at the man in her arms. His eyes stared at nothing. His head had rolled back. Her husband was dead. Gently, she lowered him to the ground. "Call 911 anyway. I've got to warn Travis. Stay here until the ambulance comes."

Pierce's face reflected his horror at having to wait with a dead man.

She had no time for his squeamishness. "Please."

Reluctantly he nodded, but he walked into the living room as he dialed the phone. The briefcase with the money still lay open on the table. She stuffed the paperwork inside and clicked it closed. She may have to explain the money to the police, but it wasn't the first thing she was going to do. Grabbing the leather satchel and the briefcase, she opened the laundry room door and wedged them between the wall and the far side of the washing machine. Next to the dryer on a hanger was the skirt and blouse she wore when she practiced being blind.

Quickly she shed her slacks and t-shirt. Blood had soaked through her clothes to stain her skin. With a wet washcloth she cleaned as much as possible. The stun pens were still in her jacket. She stuffed them into her skirt pockets.

Barefoot, she bounded up the stairs to find wedged sandals, the wig, the sunglasses and the cane. As she left through the side door, sirens blared in the distance. She made her way through two neighbors' yards before she appeared on the street. The park was only a block away. She practically ran to get there.

No one would believe she was blind the way she was going. She slowed and thought about how Rachel, her cat burglar would move. Gently, she tapped the sidewalk, grateful the city had insisted it be repaved the previous year.

At the edges of the black smoke ball, the sun was bright, and the sky was clear. Abby straightened her back and listened. Police had erected barriers preventing traffic, both vehicle, and human from entering the scene. A young officer worked to put the blockade in place. Purposely, she stumbled into a sawhorse and floundered before falling onto the street.

"Careful, ma'am. Let me help you up."

"What's happening?" she asked as he took her arm and escorted her to the sidewalk on the far side of the street."

"Car bombing."

She shook her head, mimicking a frantic look of panic. "Terrorists?"

"We don't know yet. I can have an officer help you get home if you need it."

"No. No. I'm okay. You've got important things to do."

"Yes, ma'am. A lot of people are gathering to see what's going on. You should consider a guide dog."

Interesting how men seemed to think a dog would solve a blind woman's problems. But this was a policeman. She reeled back her retort and humbly nodded. "I'm on a waiting list."

She wanted to cut across the grass but wasn't sure if she'd been truly blind, she would have dared risk being off the sidewalk. Like many Portland parks, trees dominated the landscape. She took an angled path toward a fountain in the center of the park. A homeless woman pushing a shopping cart circled the fountain. A low angry voice reached her.

Abby slowed. She wanted to double back to the gathered crowd to approach from the rear. How to do that and still appear blind?

The homeless woman was agitated. Her movements were sharp, her words edged with near violent intent, but her tone was subdued. She wasn't mumbling or talking to herself. Metal gleamed near her ear. A Bluetooth. The woman was having a conversation and keeping her voice purposely low. Abigail strained to hear, but could only pick up an occasional word, which wasn't helpful.

As she imagined a blind woman would, she stretched her hand, hunting for one of the numerous benches that surrounded the fountain and dropped onto the seat. The woman gave her a brief glance but returned to her call and her circling.

Abby tilted her face upward, seeking the sun while allowing her to watch the woman through the narrow slits of her eyes. The woman neared, her voice raised as she argued with the person on the other end of the end.

"I know they're erecting a tent in the way. Keep moving until you see the car. I heard an ambulance siren. That means there's a body."

She jerked her cart as she crossed in front of the bench. As she walked away, Abby stared at her clunky shoes to note the limp. Where was Travis? The woman worked with someone in the crowd. Maybe more than someone.

Abby glanced around. The busy park was practically deserted. Everyone was clustered near the car bombing. She and the homeless woman were the only ones present.

The other woman had stopped talking and stared off into the distance. Abby kept the woman in her sight. Was she going to leave?

But after a few minutes she gave the cart a shove and resumed her circling. Abby held her breath. It was one thing to write about a brave woman – it was another thing to be one. Timing was essential.

Not yet. Not yet. Not yet.

The woman's circles grew larger until she passed almost directly in front of her. Tentatively, Abby rose to her feet, then stumbled forward. Her cane flew out of her grasp, and she crashed to her knees. A cry of pain escaped her lips. Gasping for breath, she made no attempt to get up.

A hand wrapped around her arm. "Are you

okay?"

Abby had a flash of guilt. How mean was it to take down someone trying to help you? She hesitated. Then James' face with his non-seeing eyes came to her. Reaching up, she clasped the woman for support and struggled to her feet.

"Thank you," she said as the other woman picked up her cane to hand to her. Abby jabbed the stun pen into the woman's side. The woman was thrown to the ground, shaking like a leaf in a storm.

Abby pulled trash out of the woman's shopping cart, plastic bags filled with empty coke cans, a couple of blankets, and an incredible number of plastic bags, newspapers, magazines, a smelly pile of clothes that consisted of a jacket, three pairs of socks and gargantuan pair of pants. When the cart was empty, she lined the bottom with a blanket.

The woman was dead weight, but Abby managed to fold her body into the cart, leaving her legs dangling over the side. She grabbed the woman's hands and stretched the plastic bags into a rope to tie them behind her. Once the rope was secured to the shopping cart, she covered the woman with clothes and blankets.

Whatever didn't fit in the cart, Abby stuffed into a park trash can. When she returned, movement and a muffled scream alerted her to the woman's return to consciousness. Abby looked around to make sure they were still alone, then dug through the blankets and other garbage and used the stun pen again before the woman could overthrow the cart and escape.

When the woman was quiet, Abby wheeled her into the trees. Unsure how long it would take her to find Travis she frisked the woman's pockets, snagging her cell phone, Bluetooth, and car keys.

This time she gagged her and tied her ankles together.

"I don't have the time for this," she whispered to the unconscious woman. She covered her entire body with another blanket, then dodged through the trees in an effort to cover some ground before she had to resort to being sightless again.

Chapter Twenty-Four

Detectives Sam and Grant joined Austin and Travis in the crowded surveillance van, Tyrone located near the park. Each man folded himself onto uncomfortable chairs to see the two computer monitors, Austin operated and watched a man dressed in a worn overcoat and knitted cap inch his way closer to the police tape.

"That's got to be one of our guys. Look at his boots. Totally wrong for the homeless image he's projecting," Travis said. "Plus he's too interested in ascertaining the details."

"He's not doing anything illegal," Sam told his brothers. "We can't arrest him without cause."

The tent set up for the police, combined with the emergency vehicles, made it difficult to see anything but the flames licking the tree branches. Water wasn't squelching the fire, but the firemen worked to keep it from spreading. Two or three people parked close to the fire argued with police to get permission to move their vehicles.

The crowd pressed closer despite the flames and the police tape. The bomb squad stood off to one side waiting for the car to stop burning.

An officer gestured for their suspect to back away. When the man wanted to argue, another officer appeared. Sam leaned closer to the monitor. "Why's he still here?"

"Because a body hasn't turned up yet." Travis also wanted to know if the SUV had an occupant. If Weatherby had gotten away, there was only one place he would have gone − back to Abby's. "Does the fire department know if there's anyone inside the car?"

Sam pressed his cell to his ear then spoke in a low voice for a few minutes. "The vehicle appears to be empty, but there's a blood trail through the bushes that vanishes on the other side."

Travis scratched his jaw. "I'll check on Abby though I think she's safe with him."

One of the monitors dinged. Austin whirled in his chair, his fingers racing over the computer keyboard. "We've got a facial recognition hit and it's female." As the pixels aligned themselves into a recognizable face, everyone murmured the word shit as Abby in sunglasses and a blonde wig appeared on the screen.

"What's she doing here?" Austin asked.

Travis had already bolted from his seat and was at the rear door. "She wouldn't have come if it weren't important. I'm going to go find her. Keep an eye on our suspect."

He double-stepped without breaking into a run not wanting to attract undue attention.

Abby was on a path moving away from the tree line. It pleased him that she'd circled behind the crowd.

He approached from the side and was practically on top of her before she knew he was there. "You've got a problem with your shoe."

She knelt, and he hunkered down beside her.

"Thank goodness, I've found you," she whispered.

"What happened?" Despite her wig and sunglasses, her face was flushed, and a fine sheen of sweat dotted her upper lip.

"Jonas said a remote control set the bomb. The killers are still here, making sure he's dead."

"That's what we figured. Is Jonas okay?"

"No." Her voice cracked.

Travis stroked her bare arm in an attempt to offer her comfort when he wanted to pull her into arms. "Pierce is waiting for the ambulance, but Jonas's wounds were too great."

Too great? "He's dead?"

Her head jerked up and down. He no longer cared who saw them. He wrapped an arm around her shoulders.

But Abby, being Abby, pulled away and whispered, "Not now."

They both rose. He hovered close as he scanned the crowd. No one was paying any attention.

"His last words were to tell you...'Taggart'."

"Is that a name?"

"I think so."

"We've got a man we're watching, but the only facial shots we have of him are from your camera phone. We're not getting a positive hit, so our hands are tied."

She clamped her teeth together and pulled back the corners of her lips in a way that made her look guilty. "I have an idea. Can Austin hear what I'm saying?"

"Yes."

"There was a woman with a limp, pretending to be homeless. I grabbed her phone. Her last call was to someone she told to get nearer to the explosion. If your guy answers the phone, it means he's the one."

Travis's heart stopped. He yanked the ear bud to prevent anyone from hearing his next question. "Abby," he whispered, barely able to form the words. If Sam or Grant heard her confess to a crime, he couldn't prevent her from going to jail. "Did you kill the woman?"

Indignation gleamed as she rolled her eyes. "Of course not." She frowned at him. "But I did use the stun pen. Twice."

A gush of air escaped his lungs. The woman was probably long gone, but Abby had at least snagged her phone. He pushed the earbud back in place, only to hear Austin asking over and over, "Are you there? Are you there?"

Abby pulled the phone from her pocket and swiped her finger across the face. She'd taken no precaution with her fingerprints which were all over the phone, but Travis couldn't reverse history.

"I'm here. We're going to dial the phone now." He nodded.

Abby pushed the call button. She held the phone away from her ear so he could hear the phone as it rang and rang again. Finally, a voice said. "I told you not to call me."

"Anything?" Abby demanded, pitching her voice lower.

"Who is this?"

She hadn't fooled him. Blood drained from her face as she scrambled to disconnect. For a woman with confrontational skills, he was amazed she thought the phone would bite back.

In Travis's ear, Sam said, "Okay, we got him." Travis turned his attention back to Abby. "You did good."

She gave him a weak smile, and he grinned in return to bolster her spirits.

"Where did you leave the woman?"

She gestured behind her. "In the woods."

He rose and offered her a hand up. "Let's go find

her."

"You want an officer?" Sam asked.

Travis curled an arm around the miraculous woman he loved. "I doubt if she's still there. Abby only stunned her. She's probably recovered and long gone.

Abby pushed away from him and fisted her hands on her hips. "I tied her up."

Travis searched her face, surprised that she'd thought to do that. "And securing someone so they can't runoff is harder than I thought."

"Yeah, Sam. You need to join us."

"On my way."

Sam arrived with two uniforms. "I can hardly wait to see this in your next book."

Abby shook her head. "I'm through with mysteries. From now on I'm going to write about people who don't have murderers in their lives – women whose biggest worry is what color of flowers to plant in their garden. I could never do what you do for a living."

Sam gave her a sideways glance. "Except you're a natural. Who else would have thought to grab her phone? That was pure brilliance."

"I have her car keys, too."

He laughed and Travis joined him.

"Of course, you do." Sam held out his hand. Abby dug into the pocket of her skirt and handed him the keys.

He passed them off to one of the uniforms. "Find the vehicle and have it towed into evidence. We'll get the forensics' team on it."

The shopping cart was exactly where she'd left it.

Sam pulled back the blanket. "Well, well. If it isn't our little serial assassin. I'm sure you know the drill, but Officer James will read you your rights."

Sam stepped away as the uniformed officer stepped nearer to the cart. "Nice job."

"It took two tries."

The officer cut the plastic ties and hoisted the woman out of the cart. Once on her feet, the woman glared in Abby's direction. Travis stepped between them to prevent a vitriolic spiel sure to give her nightmares.

Abby looked up at him with weary eyes. "I need to go home."

"I'll take you."

Sam punched Travis's arm in brotherly affection. "Since she seems to be doing all the heavy lifting, you want me to send Austin to walk you back?"

Austin hooted through the earpiece. "Apparently we've acquired another member of the team who's showing all of us up."

The surge of anger caught Travis by surprise. He didn't mind the razzing from his brothers, that was to be expected, but what caught him off guard was his sense of failure. Abby should be able to depend on him, not think she had to take care of herself. Otherwise, she wouldn't stay.

"Knock off the comedy routine."

Her head popped up, and her intelligent eyes studied his face. His tone had been harsher than he'd intended. "We still have to figure out who Taggart is. Meet us at Abby's in ten."

Sam glanced at his watch, before surveying the situation. In response, he gave a curt nod. Travis struggled with internal rage. He grabbed her arm and tugged.

Chapter Twenty-Five

So the other shoe had finally dropped. Travis was furious, and she was the cause. His attempt to pull her along had her seeing red. And for a blind woman that was saying something. She dug her heels into the ground and jerked her arm away from him.

"Touch me again and you'll find out what it feels like to be on the receiving end of a stun pen."

His eyes narrowed as his lips thinned into a grimace. Maybe waking the angry giant lurking inside the gentle bear hadn't been such a good idea. Would he strike her? Better she should know now.

She raised her chin. He'd better make that first punch a good one because it would be the only shot he ever got.

A startled look replaced his anger. He gawked in disbelief. As understanding dawned, he shook his head vehemently. "I'm not mad at you. I shouldn't have grabbed you like that." His face took on a pained expression. "I'm sorry."

Sam stepped closer. "Do you need some help?"

Abby wasn't sure to whom he offered aid, but she didn't need it. Ignoring the interruption, she demanded, "Who, then? 'Cause you are definitely angry."

Travis threw his arms upward in a frustrated manner. "You make it impossible for me to protect you, running off, half-cocked, throwing yourself into the line of fire."

This macho thing had gone too far. Protective was one thing. Hyper-possessive was another. "I see. So the 'we're a team' speech means we are only a team as long as I'm the dependent one? Are you trying to make me into a woman who can't function without your help?"

Out of the corner of her eye, she saw Sam back away. Apparently she'd crossed a line, and his help was being withdrawn.

"I love the fact you're smart and self-reliant." Travis's voice was incredulous. "But this isn't a scene where you can write the ending the way you want it. We're playing an intricate game, like chess. You have to understand what each piece does and be able to predict the next move."

She sensed his helpless frustration, but he understood nothing about the teamwork of a relationship if this was what he thought.

Slapping a flat palm against his chest, she leaned closer, lowering her voice to barely above a whisper. "If this is a chess game, then the one thing you should have been able to predict is that the queen always protects the king."

Just telling him wasn't enough. Every nerve in her body screamed for revenge, for the lost years, and for the injustice she'd suffered. In all that time, she hadn't been angry, just afraid. Then Travis had come along and forced a light on all those things she'd kept hidden in the shadows, freeing her. He'd saved her but wanted her dependency in return. Never again.

She slapped his chest a second time hard. Her palm stung. "In chess," she spoke loudly. Travis winced but never took his gaze from her. "The queen always protects the king – even when he thinks he's in charge."

Whirling away, she stormed toward her house. If she talked to him one-minute longer, she'd burst into angry tears he'd likely misinterpret. She was pissed, not cowed. The cross street loomed before her, and she became aware of the voices of pedestrians. She slowed and tapped her cane. While her body faltered with a self-imposed handicap, her brain raced. A new plan was in order.

Travis Stevens had simply been a mistake.

She had an ID. She had money. She could go anyplace she wanted. Why on earth was she staying here?

Chapter Twenty-Six

"That went well," Travis muttered as Abby stomped off. "Stay where you are, Austin. I'm coming to you."

"What? Why didn't you go after her?"

Of the two of them, Austin was rarely riled, but he was now. Tolerating his brother's interference was more than Travis could handle. "If she's going to leave me, let it be now."

Sam fell into step beside him. "You're an idiot."

Perfect. Everybody had joined the team. Travis pressed his lips together to keep from lashing out.

Sam ignored his silence. "She practically told you she loved you. You've been mooning after her like a motherless calf. Go after her."

They didn't understand. He'd already failed with one ex-wife. "How can I? She doesn't need me to take care of her."

Sam stopped. Travis searched his face which had taken on that same look of frustration he had as a teenager when he couldn't control his stepfather. But this time his anger was directed at him.

"Do you know why your marriage to Teresa didn't work?"

Oh, shit. Let's not go there. Teresa was none of his business, and neither was Abby, but Sam wasn't going to be quiet until he'd had his say.

"Because she needed you. After about six months, you were sick of being the only adult in the relationship."

Enough. "That's not true. She left because…" Because he spent every available hour at work. Even more than necessary. Being at home with Teresa drained him. She'd become exactly what Abby said – dependent just like his mother had been. Hell, things had gotten so bad that in order for her to dress every morning, he'd had to pick out her clothes.

His brothers wisely said nothing while he worked the situation through in his mind.

"C'mon. Let's get this done."

He and Sam reached the van and climbed in through the back door. "Do you have a clue who Taggart is?"

Austin stared at his monitor. "None. The name doesn't come up on the CIA database. No big surprise there. We need an insider."

"Aaron Cleves," Travis said naming the Assistant Deputy Chief of the FBI. The men had worked with Cleves during their time as active SEALs and had found him a standup guy, something the government didn't produce in vast quantities.

Sam frowned. "Wrong branch of government."

Austin's fingers tapped the keyboard. "I think Travis's right. This is exactly the kind of thing Cleves likes. He keeps his ear to the ground. I'll bet he'll help."

"Okay, that's settled. C'mon dude, I'll walk with you to Abby's. I need to see her husband's corpse." Sam flung his arm over Travis's shoulder, reuniting the bond that kept the three of them tight over the years. Austin gave a wave of dismissal as the two men exited the van.

Travis circled to avoid the bombed out car. "You don't think the ambulance has removed him by now?"

"With all this confusion, I doubt if the ME's have even gotten there."

Chapter Twenty-Seven

Travis mounted the steps to Abby's bedroom. An open suitcase and a stack of clothes covered the bed. This was worse than he'd imagined. He hesitated unsure how to proceed. When Teresa left him, he'd come home to an empty house. She hadn't wanted the confrontation any more than he had.

He stopped two steps from the top uncertain of his welcome.

"He doesn't know who he's dealing with." Her voice came from the closet.

The muffled words reached him before she trudged barefoot across the room and tossed a bunch of white lacy underwear on top of the tottering stack.

"Telling me I was going off half-cocked when all I did was follow his lead."

No one else was in the room. Was she on the phone?

"It was his stun pen, after all. 'Take two' he says. And then he's surprised when I used them. And furthermore I like having them and am not giving them back. He can just sue my ass if it matters to him. Half-cocked, indeed."

As he watched her stomp around the room, he bit his inner cheek to keep from laughing. Oh, man, he was going to have to work to fix this one. She was spitting angry.

"Where are we going?" He stepped gingerly across the threshold, fearing to venture too far into the room.

Abby jumped. "Quit sneaking up on me." Like a lifetime Gap employee, she snatched clothes out of the pile and folded each with sharp precision, before adding the article to her luggage. "We aren't going anywhere. At least, not together."

"Yes, we are. If you leave, I'm going with you."

"You haven't been invited."

He leaned against the door jam and crossed his arms, hoping she would buy his casual stance. "Every time you look in your rear view mirror, that'll be me on your six."

"Why? You don't think I can disappear where Taggart or anybody else won't find me? I've got cash. I've got a new ID."

And he had her fake husband to thank for helping her in that regard. "You can't use the money. You have to turn it over to the police. When everything is said and done you might get it back, but if they find the money came from an illegal enterprise, you won't."

Her eyes narrowed, and her forehead crinkled as she appraised him. "So what? I'm not without funds. I'll use my own money if need be."

Her movements slowed. No doubt her mind scrambled to put together a new scenario.

"Do you have a plan?"

She tugged on the top flap of the bulging suitcase and attempted to zip it. "Canada."

"Good call." He cautiously inched closer. "Do you need help zipping your suitcase?"

She twirled on the ball of her foot and glared. "Don't patronize me."

Throwing up his hands in innocent surrender, he said, "I'm not. Canada is out of the US database. You won't be able to use credit cards in your name, and your car's license plates will be a problem."

Like a balloon with a slow leak, she seemed to deflate. She cast her gaze downward, turned slowly and set to work on closing her suitcase again.

She tugged on the zipper. "I wasn't going to take my car. Push here." She pointed to the peaked center.

Her onslaught was weakening. If he didn't stumble over his own tongue, she might agree to stay, but he couldn't let up yet. "Have you considered a second suitcase?"

"Yes, but that's for makeup, shoes and writing stuff."

Travis took the zipper from her control and quickly sealed the bag. "We could stop by my place so you could pick up your books."

"I've read those. It's time for me to find something new."

If she was giving up her favorite books, maybe she was serious about leaving him behind as well. His stomach knotted. "Are you flying?"

She tossed a second small piece of luggage on the bed. "Train. Thought I'd rent a car with my new ID."

"So he included a credit card in your new name as well?"

Abby paused. "No. He didn't. I guess he figured the money would have to do."

"Why do you want to leave?"

The incredulous look she gave him spoke volumes.

"Because I'm bringing killers to your door." Her tone implied he was the idiot, Sam thought if she had to explain it to him. But then her look gentled. Fear clogged his throat. He wasn't sure he could hear the truth.

"If you're forced to murder somebody to protect

me, it will scar your soul for life. You'll never be the same, and I'll be responsible."

Oh, boy. He took a deep breath and lowered himself to the edge of the bed. Had he told her nothing about who he was?

No, he hadn't.

He'd been too busy being the man he suspected she wanted simply to get her to stay. Whoever said, 'the truth will set you free' hadn't been in his position, but if she was ever going to be his, she needed to know the kind of man he truly was.

"I need to tell you about my life."

"Nothing you say will convince me I'm wrong."

"I understand, but I still need to tell you."

Something about his tone must have persuaded her that what he was going to say would be ugly, because she stopped packing and came to sit next to him on the bed. She folded her hands like the good little Catholic girl he suspected she was in her heart.

"My family is messed up. My father got hooked on drugs. When he was high, he'd beat my mother in front of Austin and me to make some misguided point. My mother finally found the courage to leave him about the time I was six, but we lived in fear and moved constantly. By the time I made it to seventh grade, I'd been in fourteen different schools."

His only friend had been his brother. In order to survive, they'd watched each other's backs. With each move had come worse neighborhoods and deeper poverty.

"In Middle School the area we lived in was so rough that in order to survive I became a gang member." He skipped over the gang beatings that had forced him into joining, but he couldn't glorify his role once he was a member.

"I stole, sold drugs, whatever the gang wanted me to do. You've never asked about my tattoo. The one over my heart was a devil with a pitchfork. That was who I was. Like your husband, I also learned to kill young. It was the worst time of my life – I didn't care if I lived or died."

Her primly folded hands reached out and covered his. He forced himself to look into her eyes, brimming with pain and sorrow.

"I worked out because I knew I would eventually be shot or go to prison, and I wanted to be strong enough not to be anyone's punk. For a few years," he snorted in disgust, "my life goal was to be strong enough to survive prison."

Enough pity party. He was no longer that lost kid. He gave her an imploring half-smile. "Rod Stevens turned my life around when he started dating my mother. He believed in me when nobody else did. Rod moved us to a better neighborhood and taught me that being a man meant living an honorable life and taking care of those who are weaker."

"So when you left home you joined the military?"

He nodded. "The Navy. As did Austin and Sam."

"So you consider Sam, your brother?"

"Not by blood, but in every way that counts. He came to live with us at sixteen when his step-father beat him with a steel pipe. Rod Stevens saved his life as well. Rod's lifelong dream had been to be a SEAL, but he was wounded and discharged before that happened. The three of us honored him by becoming SEALs."

She ran her fingers through her short hair,

making it even more tousled than before. "I thought becoming a SEAL was hard."

"You have no idea. It is the hardest thing I've ever done, but I am the man Stern wanted you to believe your husband was. I didn't remove the tattoo because that time is a part of me, but as I changed, I had the design altered. The devil is now Poseidon with a trident because I conquered the sea and made it my home. It's why I live on the water."

"You've killed a lot of people?" Her voice trembled.

He twisted his hands, so they were interlaced with hers and gave her a gentle squeeze.

"I've killed to protect my country and those I love. You're right, it does scar a man's soul, but I'm not ashamed of it. When it gets down to me-versus-them, I'm perfectly okay with it being them. Evil comes at us in many forms. Protecting those around me is what I do."

An 'ah-ha' moment dawned in her eyes. "So when I tell you I'm protecting you, you're laughing inside."

The blow her words dealt was sharper than a punch to the gut. He'd spent the past four years learning to be persuasive, and yet the one time he needed words there were none to offer. The only thing he could do was to sacrifice his pride.

"I love you. You live as honorable a life on your terms as I do on mine."

"You love me?" She closed her eyes.

He prayed she was absorbing his true feelings and not thinking of ways to let him down easy.

"I do. I want to marry you."

Desperation clawed at him. He refrained from dropping to one knee because he'd already told her more than she wanted to hear.

When the brief silence that followed weighed heavily in the air, he blurted out the only words that occurred to him. "When you say you're leaving, I'll have no choice but to go with you. My body won't function if you take my heart."

He hung his head thankful neither of his brothers had heard him grovel.

"What about Taggart?"

So, that was it? She was back to business as usual. Ignore the man and maybe he'll go away? Outrage at her reaction stunned him, but he sucked in his ego and tried to answer her question in the way she might accept.

He raised his head and looked her in the eyes. "The problem with running is that you'll never be safe. Unless you want to spend your life looking over your shoulder, there are times when you have to stand your ground."

She twisted her hands in her lap. "The night I first met you, when we were in the stairwell, all I wanted to do was dry-hump your leg. But I didn't fall in love with you until I knew no matter what happened you wouldn't share me with your brother."

A smile he couldn't control kicked the corners of his lips upward. "If it had been what you truly wanted I would have agreed. But you're right – it would have been very difficult."

"Did you know when you smile these lines crinkle?" With her fingers, she traced the wrinkles that radiated from his eyes to his hairline. "You understand I'm agreeing to live with you, but I'm not ready for marriage?"

His heart lightened as he solemnly nodded. "I do."

Her smile poked holes in his soul and sunshine flooded him. "Well, it was a good thing I packed, huh?"

His throat closed. The only agreement he could master was a gruff, "Uh-huh."

But he wasn't a complete idiot, he leaned across the small gulf that separated them and kissed her to seal the bargain. With a suitcase behind them and footsteps on the stairs, there was no way he could take this further. Although he longed to kick the door shut.

Sam both cleared his throat and politely knocked, but Travis refused to take his gaze off Abby. "Yeah?"

"Sorry to interrupt."

That was a lie. Knowing Sam, his only regret was that Austin wasn't with him to give Travis shit.

Abby's manners were better than his. She hopped off the bed and said. "Come on in. I'm just finishing gathering up my stuff."

"Pierce mentioned a briefcase full of money," Sam said.

Her cheeks flamed with embarrassment. Abby busied herself by futzing with the suitcase. If she was mortified by a kiss, she definitely couldn't handle a *ménage*, but truth be told he couldn't either.

"It's behind the washing machine with the case James brought from the car."

What? What case?

"There's another case?" Both he and Sam spoke at the same time.

She looked up. "I didn't tell you that?"

Travis refused to bolt for the stairs although that was his first reaction. Sam, he noted, watched the interplay with a cop's interest. "What's inside?"

"I don't know. I didn't open it."

He lifted the suitcase from the bed to haul it downstairs. "Let's look, shall we?"

Chapter Twenty-Eight

Saturday Morning

Sam arrived at Travis's home early Saturday morning. The men gathered around the coffee table to hear the police report. The brothers had spent half the night tracing funds from the information in Jonas's satchel. Everyone including Abby, the only one who had slept, was a little punch drunk. A third pot of freshly made coffee sat on a side table.

The weather forecast had predicted flurries of sunshine, but apparently the gray sky hadn't gotten the message because the heavy thunderclouds screamed rain. An undercurrent of apprehension kept Abby from joining the men. She focused on Travis, who kept glancing over his shoulder to check on her.

She paced behind the couch, hating that nothing made sense. Not Jonas. Not Charles. Not her life. Her mistake with Jonas had been jumping into marriage. Would Travis cause her as much regret? With all heart, she hoped her judgment was correct this time.

A corner of his lip turned up in a grin, and her silly heart soared into her throat. Had she ever felt that way about husband number one? She didn't remember it if she had.

Sam settled onto the couch. The eagerness in Austin's face reflected the love these men had of their careers.

With his fingers poised above the keyboard, Austin asked, "Who's the woman?"

Sam's expression took on a lazy grin of superiority. Only brothers would lord such a tidbit over each other while working together. Abby had missed this closeness in her life.

"You're not going to believe this." The excitement in Sam's voice was barely controlled.

She stepped closer to the couch, not wanting to miss anything.

Sam's face showed signs of exhaustion but his grin at being able to impart information gave him a superficial perkiness. "Nora D'Angelo. The Colorado wife."

Austin and Travis's heads jerked up from their laptops.

"You're kidding." Travis lowered his voice and glanced over his shoulder, before patting the couch next to him to indicate she should join them. "The last woman married to Jonas."

Abby inched around the couch, watching Travis's face as he addressed her. "You and she were the only ones who survived."

Taking a scrap of paper, he drew what looked like an org chart. "Charles was the front man. It's why all the accounts were in his name. Jonas operated as the secret weapon – the reaper."

Was he kidding? An assassin as a secret weapon? "What good did that do?"

"Espionage is spy versus spy. Stewart's respectability combined with his profession meant certain powers didn't have control over him. He was able to organize the assignments and demand top dollar. Because only he could reach Jonas, no one else had the power to make a decision in the middle of an op that might get his brother killed. So they invested a lot of effort in playing a version of now you see me, now you don't."

Travis turned to Sam. "What else have you found

out?"

Sam cleared his throat as all heads in the room turned toward him. "Nora D'Angelo is not her real name, but both suspects have lawyered up."

Austin typed furiously. "Were you able to get a fingerprint check?"

"Well, that's why I'm here. Our John Doe has seared his fingerprints beyond recognition." Sam had lowered his voice to barely above a whisper. "Who do you know who routinely does that?"

"Black Adder," the three brothers said in unison.

As usual she was the only person in the room who didn't have all the details.

Sam stretched, wearing his weariness like an overcoat. "Over the phone we got the official denial, but they have agreed to send the head guy from DC to affirm it."

Travis suddenly sat straighter which sent a shiver of alarm through Abby. "DC? Hiram Lynch is coming? It means something that they're sending in the big guns." The tone of Travis' voice confirmed the seriousness of the situation.

Abby leaned forward to see his face. "Hiram Lynch? You say his name like it's important."

"The guy's renowned in the security arena. He hasn't been in the field in years, but the work and his ability to hire others has made him rich. He likes to flaunt it. Has a private jet, huge house and I hear, expensive hobbies."

"Drugs?" Abby asked in a whisper.

Travis glanced at her. "No, legal hobbies like horse racing and NASCAR."

"NASCAR's expensive?"

The three men laughed, but it was Austin who answered her question. "It is when you own the car."

Travis brought the subject to the problem at hand. "What about the woman?"

Sam laced his hands behind his head and stretched his legs. "Fingerprints don't register a match."

Austin took his fingers from the keyboard, looked out the sliding glass door and scratched his beard. "Could Black Adder's operatives be subbing out?"

Sam rose, snagged an empty cup and poured coffee before gesturing with the pot to the others. Both men shook their heads. When Abby didn't respond, he raised an eyebrow.

"No more coffee." As it was, her nerves were on edge.

She looked around the room. These men may have known more than she did, but she wrote about murders and made a good living at it. People killed for a reason. Once the motivation was clear, so was the plan. Had Jonas tried to kill Nora? Vengeance was strong motivation, but it wouldn't explain why she killed the man in the coma.

Abby wanted more information. "I need to speak to her."

"Her, who?" Travis asked, his brow knitted in concern, the way it did when he was about to rain on her parade. "Nora?"

She thrust out her chin. "Yes."

"No," both Sam and Austin spoke in unison.

Travis's gray eyes studied her. She squirmed at her exposure.

"Why?" His voice was kind. He wanted to hear her thoughts.

Her heart swelled at how hard it was for him to relinquish control. But he was trying.

"If she's lawyered up, the police aren't getting anywhere with her. What could it hurt? If we did it in an interview room, you could record the whole thing. Should trouble erupt, you'd be nearby."

Sam shook his head. "That's not going to happen. The police have rules."

Travis's expression hadn't changed. Despite Sam's words, he was considering what her idea meant.

Abby pressed. "It seems to me like you have two choices. Charge her with murder without enough information to convict, or set her free. Which is it going to be?"

Sam scowled which delighted Abby that her research had paid off.

"Let me talk to the Captain." He stepped onto the deck, closing the door behind him.

"You're not going to let her go through with this are you?" Austin turned to his brother.

Travis grinned at her. "I think it's a good idea. Besides, as she pointed out, we'll be right there if something happens."

Sam reopened the door, a grim set to his lips. "Let's go. If we're going to do this, they want it done before her lawyer shows up."

Travis nodded. "Ms. Trey Sleuth, you're on."

Chapter Twenty-Eight

"Somewhere I read only the guilty can sleep at a time like this." Abby's words were intended for Travis's ears only.

The darkened viewing room was crowded with the four of them, and an equal number of police all watching the woman sleeping so soundly she snored.

Nora's head rested on her arms folded on the steel interview table. Her face was hidden by dull strands of dishwater blonde hair. The homeless garb from the day before had not improved with an additional day's wearing. No scent seeped into the viewing room, but Abby bet she reeked.

"Why?" He called her attention back to her statement.

"Because it's a relief when they're caught, and they can finally relax."

"Sounds believable. Will you feel better if, while you are in there, we handcuff her to the chair?"

She had given hard thought on the ride to the police station about the best way to approach the woman. Cop? Lawyer? Friend? Nora had to like her, or she wouldn't talk, but how to overcome her first instinct to distrust?

A worried woman wouldn't sleep.

"No, but it might go better if she thinks I've been arrested as well. Give me a minute."

She darted down the hall to the bathroom to reapply her makeup with a heavier hand. She tugged the elastic collar of her shirt off her shoulders and stuffed the underside of her bra with tissue to propel her cleavage forward. "Round 'em up and move them out," she said to the mirror.

With an exaggerated swagger, she strolled down the hall, satisfied when two uniforms turned to watch her with suspicious cop eyes.

"I'm ready." She opened the door to the viewing room.

"Shit," all three brothers spoke as one. The one lone holdout, Grant Matthews, grinned.

"Grant, take me in." She snapped some authority into her voice to avoid their usual reminders she wasn't competent to be left alone.

Travis's eyes held an unspoken warning Abby read without difficulty and knew his brothers not only understood the message, but were prepared to enforce it.

"Ignore him," she said to Grant, grateful he wasn't related. "I need you to be a little rough."

His sharp eyes narrowed as he followed her out of the room. "If I get killed for manhandling you, I expect flowers at the funeral."

"If this goes south, we'll both need them."

They reached the door with the innocuous sign – Interview Room One.

"Are you ready?"

Words failed her as she summoned her courage. All she managed was a terse nod.

Grant clutched her upper arm and jerked back and forth with enough force to make the teeth rattle in her head.

"Stop fighting me," he ordered, his voice loud enough to be heard on the other side of the door.

He opened the door and shoved her through, stopping only long enough to take a survey of the room and the woman who had woken enough to raise her head.

"Perfect," he snarled as though Nora being in the same room surprised him. "You two were made for each other." He thrust her into a chair across the table from the other woman who blearily followed their drama. "Married to the same guy should make you two ideal prison cellmates. Hell, you were probably working together."

"What do you mean?" Abby raised to voice and added a level of panic she hoped came through. "Why don't you listen to me? I didn't kill Jonas."

"Yeah, I could tell you were really torn up about his death since I found you in bed with another loser."

"I hadn't seen that rat bastard in years."

"He was still your husband." He peered across the table to sneer at the woman who looked remarkably unconcerned. "And yours. He may have been a bigamist, but he didn't deserve to be car bombed."

Abby turned to Nora and leaned across the table, praying she looked menacing. "You were married to Jonas?"

Grant slammed the door behind him as he left.

A moment of panic seized Abby. She was to be left alone with a killer.

Nora yawned, showing a mouth full of gold dental work. "Yeah. What of it?" She dropped her head back onto her arms.

Abby was incensed at her casual regard. How dare the woman not take her seriously?

"That cheating bastard!" She hollered just to get a reaction.

"It doesn't sound like you were burning the torch of fidelity," Nora murmured into her arms.

Abby jumped from the chair, stomped to the door

and pounded on it. "Hey, we need water in here."
Then stormed back toward her seat.

"Don't do that." The woman raised her head at
Abby's actions. "It's worse when they're here."

"I'm not staying. They can't hold me. Screwing
around isn't a crime." She turned toward the door
screamed, "I had nothing to do with his death."

She needed the woman to wake up and get mad.
Angry women blurted things they shouldn't. Whirling
on the woman, she pointed. "If you were living with
him, you murdered him."

Nora huffed out a disbelieving snort. "I hadn't
seen him for a couple of years." Finally, her face
summoned some scorn. "Since he tried to kill me."

Abby rose from her chair, leaned across the table.
Eyes wide, she whispered, "He tried to kill you?
How?"

"That's not important. Rumor is he killed all his
ex-wives. How'd you survive?"

"His brother liked me." She allowed a smile and
thrust out her chest as though no man could resist her
assets. Abby was sure that behind the soundproof
glass wall Travis groaned.

"Right, like you've got something unique." Nora
guffawed. "He only married women to lead the
government on a goose chase. I can't believe you
bumped-uglies with Charles."

She refused to let her body react to that thought.
Instead, Abby countered, "How'd you survive?"

"Fluke accident. Broke my leg in three places. It
was months before I could walk again."

Well, that explained the limp. "Wow."

Nora stretched. Her movement fanned the air

with a hygiene stench that had Abby turning her head. "How'd you meet Charlie?"

"Charlie?" Voice recognition software could place her at the scene of his death. "His brother? He showed up at my apartment one day."

"Heard he was a limp dick." Scorn filled Nora's voice.

Had Abby known the truth of that question, she might have responded. But another thought occurred to her. This woman knew more about Jonas and his history than he confided. Plus he was unlikely to have called his brother a limp dick. Someone else kept this woman informed.

Abby slapped her hand on the table and leaned into snarl, "Who told you that?"

A look of triumph crossed Nora's face. "My uncle. Probably the only true thing he ever told me, since he failed to mention my loving husband would try to kill me."

Eww. "Your uncle knew Jonas?"

Nora looked around as though she'd said too much. "Do you think they're recording this?"

"I doubt it. Some robber barricaded himself and a slew of hostages in a bank a few blocks from here. The cop who picked me up was swearing a blue streak when he had to bring me here before he joined the action. But it's probably better you don't say anything, just in case they are. They told me anything I say can be used against me in court." *Please, God. Make her believe I don't really want to know. I'm just passing time.*

"They say that to everybody. And no matter what I say I'll never go to court. I know too much."

Really? Then why did you lawyer up? "Whadda you mean?"

Nora glanced at a bare wrist and frowned. "People will get me out of here."

No watch. No phone. The woman was feeling out of her element. Good.

"Me, too? Can they get me out?"

"Why? According to you, you haven't done anything. Without proof, the police will have to release you." Nora stretched back in her chair, oblivious to her surroundings. "How'd you meet Jonas anyway?"

Abby grinned and infused perky into her persona. "At a party. He was so much fun."

"Are you kidding me? He was a moody bastard with a hair trigger."

Abby shrugged as though that didn't matter. "At times. Why'd you marry him if you thought that?"

Once again, the girl looked around. "Just did."

Abby hazarded a guess. "Your uncle made you."

"Shut up." Nora lowered her voice. "What kind of idiot are you that you just blurt out stuff like that?"

"Sorry." She leaned across the table. "Your uncle is the one who will get you out of here?"

"I doubt it. He's going to be mad, but my brothers will come as soon as I can call them."

"How come he's mad?"

"Cause I had a certain job to do, then I was supposed to leave, but I didn't."

"Didn't leave or didn't do the job?"

"Leave. When someone tries to kill you, you don't forgive. I saw an opportunity to get revenge, and I took it."

"You killed Jonas?" Abby hoped they were getting this because both women were reduced to whispering.

Nora jerked back. "Of course, not."

Abby laughed. "Yeah, you did, and not only did you do it. but if he walked through that door right now, you'd kill him again. But this time I'd help. The cheating bastard."

Nora shook her head. "You don't know who you're up against. Cause if my uncle hears I've screwed this up, I stand as good a chance of being shivved in jail as I do of walking out. Believe me, he wouldn't hesitate to kill you, too."

Abby clapped her hands like a delighted child. "Man, oh man. I can see this as a movie."

A grin slowly curled Nora's lips.

"Megan Fox could play you. I'd say Angelina Jolie, but she's too old."

Nora laughed but shook her head. "Anna Paquin, the woman who plays Sooki Stackhouse would be better. She's blonde."

"Perfect. Who plays that wolf in the program? He could be Jonas."

"No way, he's way too good-looking. But he's hairy enough." Both women hooted.

Abby sobered. "Your uncle should be sinister, like Peter Coyote or..."

Nora had grasped the idea firmly. "No. He's more teddy bear-like. Brian Dennehy could play him."

Abby bobbed her head wanting Nora to assign character roles as much as possible. "Okay. You mentioned brothers. How many?"

"Three."

"Big muscular types?" For some unknown reason, Abby gestured as though Nora wouldn't have understood the words.

"Yeah."

She scrunched up her face as she thought about the right actors. "How about the Australian guy, who played Thor? And he's got two brothers." When Nora nodded, she pushed a little harder. "Okay, so here's the story. Everybody loves the uncle, but he has a secret."

"More like a secret life."

Abby grinned. "Even better."

C'mon pick up this storyline. You already know what happened. Tell me.

She tilted her head as Nora spoke, "Jonas also has secrets. So my uncle sends me to find out Jonas' secrets. Of course, that means sex."

"Ooh, heavy seduction scene." Abby laugh sounded a little wooden, but the other woman didn't notice.

"Yeah, but then he tries to kill me by drugging me and stuffing me into a car which he pushes off a cliff."

Inwardly Abby gasped. Travis had been right. She had barely escaped with her life.

"My body is thrown free, but my leg is broken, and I can't crawl away."

"Kind of like that movie, *127 Hours*," Abby struggled to keep her tone normal.

"Exactly. Except I have my cell phone. My brothers rescue me, and I recoup for eight painful months." She stopped, her face lost in memories.

Abby waited before impatiently asking, "What happened next?"

Before Nora could respond, the door swung open, and Travis glowered at her. "You." He pointed.

"Come with me."

Really? She was so close. He couldn't have waited five more minutes? But his expression convinced her he wouldn't take 'no' for an answer. She rose from the chair and sashayed toward him, trying to maintain the fictional character she'd invented for the other woman's benefit.

When she looked back, Nora's face had lost its animation, and she'd turned on the bored I-don't-give-a-damn expression. Whatever she might have told Abby was gone.

Chapter Twenty-Nine

Once the door to the interview room was firmly closed, Travis wrapped his arms around Abby, hoping to quench the fire in her eyes. "You did great, but we've got to get you out of here."

She wedged her hands between their chests and pushed against him. He eased his grip, trying to appear calm. He'd fought against his every instinct letting her go alone into the interview room.

Abby's firmed lips assured him she was annoyed he'd pulled her out. "I didn't get enough information. You came too soon."

Her determination was admirable, but while she had been busy, Aaron Cleves from the FBI called Austin with bad news. Robert Taggart "RT" Lytle had a federal warrant for the brother and sister being held in the Portland jail, and his plane had landed an hour ago.

"Do we pull her out now?" Sam cared about getting the information like every officer in the room, but Travis knew he'd stop the interview in a heartbeat if needed.

He had shaken his head and hoped he was right. "Not yet, she's getting good stuff."

"Yeah, she is."

Austin slapped the table while peering at his laptop. "Pull her out now."

Travis jerked his head away from the glass. "Why?"

"I just got a feed from the surveillance camera in Charles Stewart's basement. Abby's been pinpointed. Look at this guy, studying the photos of her on the wall."

"Taggart?" Sam asked.

"Who else could it be?" Travis studied the monitor. "Do you have a time stamp on this?"

"Thirty minutes ago. He could here by now."

Travis had sworn under his breath as he'd raced down the hall to retrieve Abby, who now stood in front of the door, arguing with him.

"Believe me, you got plenty." He started to grab her arm and tug but held himself back, knowing how much she hated being herded. "We've got to hurry."

He gestured toward her coat draped over a chair. She was quick. Without another word, she snatched the coat and headed for the elevator.

The elevator was not empty. Once inside, he helped her into her hooded jacket, standing close.

"Why?" she asked, keeping her tone low.

"Not now. In the car. Pull up your hood."

Downtown parking had been difficult to find. They'd chosen the closest covered parking garage a few blocks away. A sprinkling rain forced pedestrians to walk quickly. No one bothered with an umbrella, but Abby's hood appeared normal. Travis kept her body between the building and his. He would have felt more comfortable if he'd been able to draw his gun.

She must have sensed his urgency because she kept pace with him despite his long strides and said nothing.

At the corner, they waited in a small, tight group to cross the street. "You know," she said. "This is just like a game of chess."

He didn't want to lose his concentration, but to be polite he asked, "How so?"

"There is no free will in chess. You have to move

whether you want to or not or you forfeit the game."

He nodded. The crowd surged forward. Out of habit he reached for her arm, but she wasn't beside him. He whirled to see she'd crossed behind him.

"What are you doing?"

"You're right-handed. If something happens, you won't want me in the way."

Once again, in the midst of a crisis, she'd managed to surprise him. If he had to pull his gun, he might have hesitated because she was there. His tension evaporated as her words settled him. Abby was a partner, not a liability. He allowed himself to sink into battle-ready alertness as in his combat days.

The dark gray sky heralded the advent of a serious storm. They took cover in the parking garage, which despite the half-open walls, was as dark as a cave. His eyes took a moment to adjust. His head told him they were safe, but his nerves didn't agree. He expanded his senses but saw nothing out of place.

Abby pushed the elevator button. Nothing happened, indicating it was close. He scanned the garage behind them for a second time. His neck tingled in that familiar way which always predicted danger.

A siren screamed in his head. He barked, "Stairs," then grabbed Abby, wrapping her in his arms and lifting her off the ground.

Fortunately, she offered no resistance, as he had no time for explanations. Her fashionable boots weren't meant for racing. They'd barely reached the steps when he heard the shout behind them.

"That's her."

A quick glance confirmed his worst fears,

Taggart, flanked by Nora's other two brothers, fumbled for weapons as they raced toward them. Side-by-side, Travis and Abby took the steps two at a time. At the second-floor landing, he pulled her into the garage and dropped to the concrete between rows of cars.

From his boot, he produced a second gun, flipped off the safety and handed it to her. "Wait here. Shoot to kill," he whispered, praying she had the resolve to squeeze the trigger without closing her eyes.

She scooted between the wall and a car, nodding. Her look reflected a steely determination as though she encountered killers every day. The shuffling of boots on concrete and whispered voices convinced him he had to get the men away from Abby's hiding place.

He dug a flash bang out of his pocket and tossed it over the vehicle. The explosion was blinding. Travis took off at a dead run.

Chapter Thirty

Abby was grateful for the shield of the car when the place lit up like daylight. Travis had sprung to his feet and taken off running. Shots rang out interspersed with shouted commands. The gun weighed heavy in her hands as she attempted to reason through her next action. But her thoughts were, so jumbled nothing made sense.

Without him telling her, she knew this had to be Taggart. But the words that filled her with panic were 'that's her' not 'that's them.' They were after her. Without Travis, she was as good as dead. Avoidance was impossible. She had to be as tough as he was, or she'd get them both killed.

In a moment of unexpected silence, she heard the quiet shuffling of shoes. Not all the men had followed Travis. She struggled to produce enough moisture to wet her lips before lowering her upper body to peer under the car. A sea of concrete stretched before her, but no shoes.

"Come on out. I know you're here," a soft voice called, sounding more concerned than sinister.

He was close - only a car or two away. She angled her head in the direction of the sound.

Nora's words haunted her. Everybody liked her uncle, but he was desperate. Otherwise, he wouldn't be here. Others hadn't handled it the way he wanted. The man stalking Abby was a killer, and she'd do well to remember that.

She wiped first one sweaty palm, then the other on her jeans and tried not to think what would happen if he found her before Travis returned. Shots rang out in the distance, but her focus was on the soft footsteps and quiet voice too near for comfort.

She bent a second time to search under nearby cars. It was then she saw the expensive wingtips. Maybe it was the cuffed trousers that clued her in, but this guy was Agent Stern in a gentler pose.

That thought steeled her resolve. Twelve years in a marriage that was really a prison. If push came to shove, she would not willingly step back into a hell of somebody else's making.

She flattened herself and slid under the car. Waves of cold emanated from the concrete, which helped cool her down. But once the pavement had sucked the heat from her body, only cold sweat remained. From her position, she watched the footsteps head toward the hood. She slid further underneath, so he couldn't see her unless he laid flat on the concrete.

His footsteps stopped. Abby listened for telltale sounds of what was happening. Boots hitting the concrete were running toward them. It might be Travis, but she'd never heard him make a sound when he moved so that could be one of the brothers.

The wingtips tilted and immaculately pressed trousers knelt on the concrete before her. She didn't have to aim to hit him. All she had to do was prop the gun on the ground and squeeze the trigger.

"Abby." Travis's voice sounded panicked, but worse he'd identified his location.

She concentrated on keeping her eyes open and gently squeezed the trigger like he'd shown her. Not once, not twice, but three times. Blood spurted from Taggart's leg. A sharp cry of pain, followed by more weapons firing.

In the distance sirens screamed.

Abby scooted from under the car, crouching behind a tire. Her hands shook, but she didn't let go of the gun. Her stomach lurched as she swallowed bitter bile. She refused to give in to nausea.

She closed her eyes. And then Travis was there. Prying her fingers off the gun. Holding her. Murmuring in her ear. Wrapping her in his protective arms.

"It's okay. Cry it out."

She hated crying, but she buried her head in his chest and let the tears fall.

He leaned close to allow her to hear his words and the worry in his voice.

"I thought I'd lost you when I realized Taggart hadn't followed me."

She hiccupped, but forced herself to stop sobbing. "I shot his leg."

An abrupt laugh erupted, making his chest rumble. "Yes. You did. You, clever, clever woman. That saved our lives."

She lifted her head to look into his cloudy gray eyes. "How did Taggart know where we were?"

"Our cameras picked him up in Stewart's secret basement office," Travis said. "When his nephews showed up, we figured they were on their way down here to get Nora and her brother out of jail. At the same time, the FBI arrived at the airport. Apparently Taggart had been running his own espionage agency for years. When the FBI started an investigation, he had to take care of loose ends — like Stewart and your husband."

The sound of sirens now blared to indicate how close they were. Travis rose, lifting her with him and raising one hand as the police car squealed to a halt in front of them.

He settled her on the trunk of the car. "I need to talk to the police. Wait here."

But he didn't walk away. His hand was wrapped around her leg as he spoke to the uniformed officer and gestured his instructions. Sam and Austin showed up with a tall lanky man in tow.

Both brothers approached. "You okay?" Austin asked.

Sam clasped her chin and turned her head to see her eyes. "Do you want to go the hospital?"

"No. I'm fine."

Travis scooped her into his arms and announced, "I'm taking her home. You know where to reach us."

"I can walk."

"I'll let you walk, but you're never leaving my sight again."

Abby rolled her eyes and pressed her lips tight to keep from smiling, but her heart thrilled with happiness at feeling safe and whole together. She loved this man, and she was free. Free to spend the rest of her life being cared for by someone who truly loved her.

Five days of hell had freed her from twelve years of prison.

And she had a really good idea for a new story.

THANK YOU!

Thanks for reading The Wrong Hero, the second book in the Wrong Series where Wrong Never Felt So Right. I truly hoped you enjoyed it.

If you liked this book, tell a friend, write a review, or send an email. If you hated this book, tell me why. Let me know where I failed to value your time. I welcome any comments you would like to make.

If you would like to be notified of the next book in this series. Please go to my website at: www.Nancybrophy.com and sign up for my newsletter. Or you can email me at: Nancybrophy@gmail.com. I appreciate hearing from readers.

Made in the USA
Charleston, SC
21 December 2015